GET OFF MY CASE!

MOTHER VS SON – THE FLIP SIDE

GET OFF MY CASE!

MOTHER VS SON – THE FLIP SIDE

JOHN FARMAN

Piccadilly Press • London

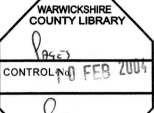

First published in Great Britain in 2003
by Piccadilly Press Ltd.,
5 Castle Road, London NW1 8PR

A catalogue record for this book is available from the British Library

ISBN: 1 85340 718 6 (trade paperback)

3 5 7 9 10 8 6 4 2

Printed and bound in Great Britain by Bookmarque Ltd
Typeset by Textype Typesetters
Cover design by Fielding Design
Set in 11/16 pt Palatino and Courier

Hans Across the Sea

'Matt, are you there? Supper's on the table.'

'Matt, are you coming down, Charlie and I have nearly finished.'

'MATT!'

'. . . Ah, there you are. What have you been doing?'

'Uh?'

'I asked what you've been doing. I rather hoped it was homework.'

'Yeah, something like that.'

'What like that?'

'Oh I don't know, just stuff.'

'What sort of stuff?'

'Stuff. You know. Look, I don't ask you and Charlie what you've been up to every five minutes, do I?'

'That's because you don't care.'

'And who bloody asked you, Charlie?'

'Somebody's got to stick up for Mum. She's only asking because she's worried about you.'

'Well, aren't you Mummy's good little girl then.'

'OK, you two, I think we'd better not go any further with this. Charlie, darling, what sort of a day did you have?'

'Brilliant, thanks Mum. All the prefects had lunch in the staff dining-room today. They're thinking of doing it regularly as a sort of way of finding out what the general feeling is amongst the kids.'

'Like spies?'

'No, Matt. It's supposed to bring the whole school closer together.'

'Bollocks, all it'll do is make us hate the prefects even more. You'll be lucky if anyone talks to you.'

'Just because you think you're such a nonconformist. Not everyone feels like that. Some of us want to make school the sort of place we can be proud of.'

'Proud of! Are you kidding? How can you be proud of a dump like that. They make up about ten new useless rules every day.'

'And you break about nine of them. Anyway, you have to have rules. If you had your way there'd be total anarchy.'

'So?'

'She's right, Matt. You have to have some sort of order.'

'Yeah Mum, of course. Might have guessed you'd agree with her. You always do.'

'That's not true. You come out with such daft things.'

2

'How do you know it would be daft? They've never tried it.'

'Look, this is getting nowhere. Matt, finish your food, then get upstairs. '

'Suits me.'

'And do your homework.'

```
From: 'Matt' <mattmason@coolmail.com>
Date: Friday 26th April
To: hans@coolmail.com
Subject: My Hard, Hard Life
```

Hi Hans,

Long time no e-mail. Must be four days. How's Hamburg, you lucky Germanic person? Sounds like you're not missing this place at all. Two years over here is long enough for anyone, I'd say. Wish my old man would get a job abroad. Mind you, since his new 'her indoors', he probably wouldn't take me anyway. Is Krautland really as cool as you say? Anything new on ze Fräulein front?

Life here's pretty crappola as per usual. You asked me about prison — sorry — school. I tell you, if everyone was doing as bad as me they'd have to close the bloody place down — no bad thing, I think. Some don't see it that way. Mum for instance. She's giving me real grief about my progress (or lack of it). The more she asks me what's up, the more I keep saying 'nothing'. Trouble is, even I'm not too sure I know what's wrong — just about everything most times. One of the biggest things wrong is that she keeps asking me what's wrong. Do you ever get those times when you feel everyone's on your case? I get so pissed off.

. . . and another thing:

Just lately she keeps comparing me to Charlie, the Mother Teresa of Randolph Drive. It's bloody awful having a sister who can do no wrong (especially if you can do no right). By the way, why do you keep asking about her? Don't say you still fancy her? — even Germans must have some taste.

How's your gorgeous big sister Bella been getting on without you? Surprised you didn't ask me to keep an eye on her when you all left — I'm that sort of caring guy as you well know.

Keep up the e-mails,

Matt

Two Against One

From: 'Matt' <mattmason@coolmail.com>
Date: Wednesday 8th May
To: hans@coolmail.com
Subject: War At Home

Glad you liked the piece what I wrote.
Yes, you twit, it was a joke about being
arrested for smiling outside McDonald's.

Just had another mini set-to with Mum
and Charlie. Blimey, even goldfish in
bowls get more privacy than me. Mum keeps
bleating on about homework and Miss
Aren't-I-Wonderful keeps joining in,
agreeing with everything she says. It's
not that I won't do it — I just can't get
it together. It's so bloody boring. You
know what I mean? Or do you? You were a
bit clever, as I remember! Anyway, what's
the fuss all about? If the big boys get
their way, we'll all be playing soldiers
before long. At least we could get to be

on the same side as you lot this time. I have it on reliable authority that no GCSEs are required to get your head blown off. Isn't that fab.

Hey. What's your new school about? What are all the other Krautlings like? I've only ever met one . . . that's you (and that was bad enough!). By the way, don't mention the war whatever you do. Stick to football and lager — that's what you lot do best. (Oh yeah — and fast motors.)

You vill reply soon, or else.

Matt

Wednesday 8th May

Had another run-in with Matt today. That's about a hundred this week. He seems to be doing no work at all these days. I reckon he'll fail all his exams at this rate, and even then we won't be able to say anything. It's like walking on eggshells whenever he's around. Practically anything I do or say seems to set him off.

Sooner or later I'm going to have to introduce the kids to Jim. I looked back in this diary and realised we've been seeing each other for over nine months now. I've tried to talk about him, but Matt shows no interest at all. I asked Jim, when we'd finished work today, if he'd like to come over for lunch on Sunday. Talk about trial by fire – he'll be the first man they've seen me with since John and I split. If Jim can put up with Matt, then he really does love me. I've warned him so many times, but he says his daughter Jodie's just the same. I can't wait for him to be able to stay over, but I'm terrified of the problems it might cause – especially with Matt.

Looks like I might get promoted to line producer on Chefs at Home. *Celia's going on maternity leave, poor dear, so I should get her job. Heaven knows, I could do with the extra money. Told Jim and he seemed really pleased. I wouldn't mind betting he had something to do with it. Doubt whether Matt could care less. He should do. Him and his sister cost more to run than I do – each!*

Who Is This Jim?

Thursday 9th May

'Matt, darling, while you're down here, can I ask what your plans are for Sunday?'

'Uh?'

'Will you be here on Sunday around midday?'

'Dunno.'

'Sorry, was that a considered reply, or some kind of animal impression?'

'Ha, very ha.'

'Look, could you turn the telly down? It's just that I've someone coming over for lunch on Sunday.'

'So? Am I on the menu or something?'

'I sometimes wish you were. No, I'd really like Charlie and you to meet him. You've heard me talk of Jim.'

'Have I?'

'Many times.'

'So? He's *your* friend, isn't he? What's it got to do with me – or us even?'

'Look, Matt. Why do you always have to be so

difficult? I just thought it might be nice to have Sunday lunch as a family – like we used to.'

'Haven't you noticed, we're not a flipping family and I've never met this bloke.'

'That's why I want you to . . . Oh hell, I give up with you.'

'I wish you would. I might be able to watch telly in peace.'

'I'm only trying to include you in things.'

'I don't ask to be, do I?'

'What's so wrong with joining in?'

'I just don't have anything to say. All you ever do is ask the same old questions.'

'Maybe you should try answering them.'

'Maybe you should try minding your own business.'

'Oh Matt, what's got into you? Every conversation we have turns into a battle these days.'

'It's not my fault. If only you'd leave me alone.'

Thursday 9th May

It's relentless. That boy's impossible. Ask him for a simple favour – to be in on Sunday – and he tries to make me look stupid. What did I ever do to deserve all this . . . and when will it end? He's like having a grumpy cuckoo in the nest who seems determined to push the rest of us out. I talked to Bryony this evening and she said her Craig's just the same.

Anyway, I can't keep staying at Jim's place and coming home at all hours, so something's got to give. If only Matt would be reasonable. Charlie'll be fine, I'm sure. She's known about Jim for quite a while and just wants me to be happy. As for Matt, I sometimes wonder if he suffered more than he ever let on from his dad going. He never said anything, but he's the sort of boy that wouldn't open up anyway. Maybe I should try having a word with John. I think that could be where the problem lies. It could be that Matt never forgave him for leaving us all. But nor did I, come to that!

From: 'Matt' <mattmason@coolmail.com>
Date: Thursday 9th May
To: hans@coolmail.com
Subject: Jim Alert!

Beware — hormones akimbo. Mum wants us to meet her bloke — Jim, I think she said. Can't think why — maybe we've got to approve of him and stuff. He's the director on CHEFS AT HOME the series she works on. Why do I have to meet him? She doesn't approve of me so why care if I approve of him? It's bonkers. Anyway, he's coming over on Sunday — for lunch apparently. I shall of course be my usual charming self (or not).

Reckon I'm heading for a right ruck with Sister Charlie the teenage nun. She's about to be made Head Girl and I know we're never going to hear the bloody end of it. Head Girl and Bottom Boy in one family — is zis possible? It's awesome, man, she almost can't help being perfect (a perfect prefect!) and I can't help being crap. Oh well, c'est la vie, as they say . . . somewhere.

Sorry, I've been rabbiting on. Did you catch Slimebag on Sky? What a band! Do you get that sort of stuff in Germany? Wicked, eh! How bad would it be to be one of those guys? Say and play what you want and the grosser you get the more everyone buys your stuff and the more the girls fancy you. Cool or what?

Sounds as if things are quite good in Krautland. Wish I was there . . . (and you were here).

Matt

Luncheon Is Served

Sunday 12th May

'Matt, are you up there? Could you come down, please?

'Matt, darling, Jim's here, could you say hello?'

'Hello.'

'*MATT!* Come down here at once and say hello properly – and don't clomp down the stairs . . .'

'Didn't I just ask you *not* to clomp down the stairs? Jim, this is Matt.'

'Hi Matt, how you doing?'

'OK – er – thanks.'

'Sorry to disturb you. Were you busy?'

'Not really.'

'I don't suppose you were doing your homework.'

'You're right there, Ma.'

'He practically lives on that computer, Jim. God knows where it will get him.'

'It sort of depends what he's planning to do. You can make a lot of money if you know your way around all

14

the software that's about these days. Have you any ideas, Matt?'

'No. Not really.'

'You told me you might want to be a journalist.'

'Yeah Mum, maybe.'

'Well either you do or you don't.'

'Yeah, either I do or I don't.'

'Jim's the series director on *Chefs at Home*.'

'Oh, right.'

'Have you seen it, Matt?'

'Mum brought home a couple of vids the other week.'

'What did you think?'

'OK, I suppose. I can't really work out why all the fuss about food.'

'It's very popular these days.'

'It's wasted on me. I'm a Big Mac and pizza sort of person.'

'Well, lunch will be ready in a minute.'

'I'm going round Dean's.'

'Oh no you're not. I asked you specially to be in today.'

'Yeah, and I said maybe.'

'Well, maybe you won't get any pocket money this week if you continue to be so rude.'

From: 'Matt' <mattmason@coolmail.com>
Date: Sunday 12th May
To: hans@coolmail.com
Subject: Mum's New Playmate

Met this Jim bloke today — the bloke Mum's
been seeing? Looks a lot younger than Dad.
Not bad clothes for an oldster — no cardi-
gans or patterned jumpers . . . or M&S jeans.
He must be doing something right, he's got
one of those new convertible Jags — they go
like hell, apparently. Why's he after my ma
though? 'Tis a puzzle to be sure. She must
have hidden charms, I suppose. Yuk, did I
really say that? Blimey, I can't even go
there. He asked me what I thought of their
programme and I was quite polite for me.
Didn't tell him I thought it was a heap of
self-important, over-cooked middle-class
poo. Actually, now I come to think about it
. . . why didn't I?

Without wanting to sound remotely homo-ish
— I'm missing you quite a bit (sweetie!).
You left me here alone to face the enemy,
while you went back to sausage-dog land —
you b****** (what's Kraut for bastard?).

Fine mate you turned out to be.

Take care,

Matt

16

Sunday 12th May

Thank God that's over. Good old Matt – predictable as ever: standard non-communication mode. It's so tiring. Though, to be fair, when he got over his initial rudeness, I don't think he actually minded Jim – especially as he seems to consider most grown-ups as aliens. Jim, bless him, seemed totally unfazed by the whole encounter – says he's met far worse than him. Where, I asked – a high-security prison? He said he was the same at his age – it's a boy thing, apparently: hated himself, hated the world and hated anyone who tried to 'understand' him. Charlie, bless her, rather approved of Jim. 'Lush' was the word I think she used. I'm not sure it wasn't because of his car! I wanted to ask Matt what he thought of Jim, but couldn't face what the little sod might say, so chickened out. Wondered if the whole thing might have put Jim off, but he seemed as keen as ever when we got back to his place!!

Wish I could find out what it is that's bugging Matt. I'm sure he's not a bad kid underneath. If anything he's got more of a moral conscience than Charlie. She makes a lot of noise about making a better world, but it's mostly just talk. It's just that Matt puts himself across so dreadfully. It's almost as if he wants people to not like him. Christ knows what will happen when he wants to get a job – if ever. As for his clothes, I give up. Everything looks as if it's ten sizes too big, and I swear

*those stupid low-slung jeans he insists on wearing –
with the crotch somewhere round his knees – must have
soaked up just about every puddle in the area. If only his
dad would have a word.*

Our Father,
Who Art Not Here

From: 'Matt' <mattmason@coolmail.com>
Date: Tuesday 14th May
To: hans@coolmail.com
Subject: Bubbles Up Your Bum

Thanks for the quick reply, even if you were showing off.

Your new house sounds awesome, man. Have you really got a Jacuzzi? Flash or what. Don't go getting bubbles up your bum, mein Herr. Mind you, I suppose there could be worse things in a strange country — you must know what foreigners are like — you are one! How's your dad's new job? Has your mum got a kitchen yet? I read somewhere that when Germans sell their houses they take the flipping kitchens with them. Is that right?

You said you've had to practically

relearn the old German. Vat a shamen-
hausen! My new favourite German word is
Geflugelfleisch-untersuchungsveriordnung,
by the way. I looked that up too. Something to do with dead chickens, I think,
but I might be wrong.

Any chance I could visit (and acciden-
tally on purpose lose my return ticket)?

Bye for now,
Matt

One hour later

'Matt, are you there? It's your father. He wants to talk to you.'

'Oh no! Do I have to? Can't he ring back?'

'No, he can't. Come down and get the phone.'

'Oh sh . . .'

'Hi Dad, how's it going?'

'Hello Matt. Fine thanks. How are things with you?'

'OK thanks.'

'That's good. How's school?'

'OK thanks.'

'Are you getting much homework?'

'Enough.'

'Good . . . Er, I haven't spoken to you for a bit – what

with Sarah and things, I've been rather busy. But you know you can always ring up for a chat.'

'Yeah, I know, Dad.'

'Good – So, er, is everything OK with you? Your mum seemed a bit worried . . .'

'Fine, thanks. If everyone left me alone, it would be even better.'

'Yes. Well . . . that's good . . . Sarah says she hopes you'll come and see us soon.'

'Yeah, OK.'

'Soon then. Give us a ring and we'll fix a date. Goooood. Well, it's been great talking to you. Love to Charlie, bye.'

'Yeah, bye Dad.'

```
From: 'Matt' <mattmason@coolmail.com>
Date: Tuesday 14th May
To: hans@coolmail.com
Subject: My Dad
```

If it isn't bad enough dealing with the Grand Controller, I just had Dad on the phone. Another earth-shattering conversation. It's bloody awful. I can tell he wants to talk, and I suppose I do too, but we just can't get it off the ground. It's a race to put the phone down first. Our record was about ten minutes, and that was after I was dragged home by the cops for being drunk and nicking that gnome from someone's front garden. Remember that party? Wicked or what!

Trouble is Dad and me don't really have anything in common. Neither of us are into sport. He only likes pipe-smoker's music (like jazz), I like heavy metal. He likes proper novels, I like fantasy stuff, he likes the country, I hate grass — know what I mean? And so it goes.

What really pisses me off is that Charlie seems to be able to chat with the old man forever. They talk bollocks for hours on end.

Thanks for inviting me over. All I have to do is get the cash together. Back to the old bank robbing again, unless you've got a spare U-Boat . . . whoops!

Matt

From: 'Matt' <mattmason@coolmail.com>
Date: Tuesday 14th May
To: hans@coolmail.com
Subject: Mr Happy

You really are Mr Happy from Hamburg,

aren't you. It's not fair, your mum and dad are great, I always thought so. You don't know what it's like to be from a broken home like what I am. There ought to be charities for me (and luxury homes where I can live forever).

It was a real drag when my dad left my mum for a younger model (actually, anything further from a model wouldn't be possible). Now I'm stuck with two gobby females, and Mum's transmuted into an alien — all hard and bossy and telling me what to do all the time.

And then there's Dad. I hardly ever see him. His loss, not mine, I reckon. Sounds like you do loads with yours. It's weird, I never asked you when you were over here. What do blokes do over there? Does it involve those funny leather shorts and hats with feathers in? I could put everything I know about Germany on the back of a stamp.

I'm lying, I meant the head of a pin.

Take care,

Matt

Tuesday 14th May

Asked John to phone Matt, but judging by the length of their conversation, it was much the same as usual. I don't know if it's just a male thing, but they seem to find it impossible to have a decent conversation.

Oh hell, only a few days to D-Day. Don't think I've been so nervous since I asked my mum about having a coil fitted. I just hope I can go through with it. Having Jim stay is sort of admitting to the kids that we're actually having sex. I'm not sure they (especially Matt) can actually cope with it. Come to that, I'm not sure I can. John never had that problem, of course. His performances were always away from home (and while we were still married, the bastard) and now he has his own house.

I'm now worried about John and Matt. Much as I hate John, I don't want him to lose touch with his son. Matt really needs a father-figure at the moment, but they seem to be drifting further and further apart. I think that Matt must think that by leaving us, his dad handed over all rights to reprimand him or even try to direct his future. In a funny way I agree, but where does that leave me? By having to be mother and father, I seem to be getting up Matt's nose every time we speak. The situation's not helped by Charlie being so much easier to get on with. Probably because she's so much less complicated.

The last thing I want to be is a cross between a

policeman and a shrink, but that's probably the only way I'm going to come out of all this in one piece. I am getting a bit fed up with being the bad guy though.

Argument 354b

'Matt, could you fill the dishwasher?'

'Do I have to – I'm watching a vid?'

'I'm afraid I gave the maid the night off. That just leaves you.'

'Why can't Charlie do it?'

'Because she's doing her homework.'

'Yeah, so I *could* be doing mine.'

'But you're not, are you?'

'I could be in a minute.'

'But you won't be, will you? Chance would be a fine thing. You'll just be up on that computer. I sometimes wish we'd never bought the damned thing.'

'It's more fun than a stupid dishwasher.'

'Why does everything have to turn into a battle of wits with you? I ask you to do a simple task and this is what I get. I sometimes wonder what you see me as, Matt? Am I just a sort of servant who's here to do your bidding?'

'I dunno.'

'Well I *do* know. I'm fed up to the back teeth running around after you. There's going to be some changes around here.'

'Why? Are we really getting a maid?'

'I'll give you a maid in a minute.'

'Right on. Could she be around seventeen, with long blon . . .'

'Matt, fill the bloody dishwasher NOW, before I lose my rag. I'm seriously contemplating going on strike. Then you'd feel the draught.'

From: 'Matt' <mattmason@coolmail.com>
Date: Thursday 16th May
To: hans@coolmail.com
Subject: Rebellion on Randolph Drive

Thanks for your e-mail. Germany sounds pretty cool to me. Mind you, anywhere apart from here sounds pretty cool. Sounds like you all live much better than we do and you always beat us at football (if not wars, ha ha!). Mind you, I don't know if I approve of everything being squeaky clean and efficient like you described. Don't think I'd fit into that too well. I'm glad that you find the girls easier to chat up. Over here they're like from another planet

— Planet Silly. The only time I ever get near one is at parties, and then you don't really talk, you just snog. So what, you're probably wondering?

Another fight with Mother Superior today. Says I never do anything round the house and that I treat the place like a hotel . . . pause for deep yawn! She's even threatened to go on strike. I wish this was a flipping hotel. I'd at least be able to get meals in my room and without going through the nightly inquisition.

Bye for now,

Matt

Thursday 16th May

They really should legalise the culling of teenage sons.

That's it. I've had enough. That bloody kid can sort out or ship out. I'm just fed up with working my arse off every day and then coming home to my other jobs – unpaid cook, butler and chambermaid, you name it – all in one. I wish someone had put all this in the instructions when I was first thinking of having babies – I'd have run a mile. Charlie's not a lot better, but at least she does things without complaining when I ask. The point is, if I do have a go-slow, he'll simply have to pull

28

his grubby little finger out or starve and walk around in filthy rags. Hang on, he does that already.

Now I think about it, his father wasn't much better either. The kitchen was like a foreign country to him, and I don't think he ever *found out where we kept the Hoover. I reckon he thought it was all done by magic. Things just cleaned themselves. I blame his mother. She hardly let him blow his nose on his own. I wonder how his new woman copes – poor cow. Good riddance, I say.*

Clean Shirt Alert!

Friday 17th May

'Mum, have you got a clean school shirt?'

'Not on me. I don't need one. Have you looked at the stuff I ironed last night?'

'Uh?'

'Sorry, Matt, I'm in a hurry. I don't have time for this. You'll have to find one yourself.'

'Do whah?'

'Find it yourself! If there isn't one there, it means you never put one in the washing basket.'

'There isn't one there – I mean here.'

'Then the one that isn't here or there, was never put in the basket, was it?'

'What do you mean? What am I supposed to do now?'

'You'll have to wear an unwashed one, I suppose.'

'But they're all in a great big pile in the middle of my room.'

'The answer's in the question. Look, don't blame me. I've told you enough times.'

'But it'll need ironing.'

'Then iron it, dear Liza.'

'Do whah?'

'Take it to the laundry room, switch on the iron, wait for it to get hot and then do what I do practically every night . . . *iron the bloody thing*.'

'But you know I don't do irons.'

'You mean you *didn't* do irons. Today might be the start of a wonderful new steamy experience.'

'Ha bloody ha.'

'Sorry, Matt, I just can't stand here arguing. I'm running late. We've a production meeting at nine-thirty . . . Bye.'

'But . . . '


```
From: 'Matt' <mattmason@coolmail.com>
Date: Friday 17th May
To: hans@coolmail.com
Subject: Housework for Men
```

```
Guess what, I had to iron my own shirt
today. Ma really did go on strike — bloody
cheek — and told me to get on with it.
What's the world coming to? You can't get
the staff these days. Doesn't she realise
that the future lead reporter of a major
national paper shouldn't be doing such
things. Actually, it wasn't that hard, but
```

I can't tell her that, can I? Don't want to give these women ideas, do we, Herr Camarade.

Glad to hear you're still OK and that you haven't been sent off the pitch for laughing. Is it true that Germans don't get jokes? I heard that their humour stops at banana skin incidents . . . please advise?

Charlie the Wonder Girl's just said that she wants to go into 'the caring business' — like a doctor or a shrink or something. It's so she can help people. What total pants. The only way she could help anyone would be to shut up. She's enough to send you to bonkerdom, not make you better! Honest, it's like living with Jesus's pushy sister. She'd better not try her psychiatry on me. It'll take more than a session with her Holiness to cure me.

Any news about when I can come over? I could probably get the fare out of Mum. She'd be glad to get rid of me, ha ha.

Not missing you at all,

Matt

Friday 17th May

I really believe I got one over on Matt this morning. Instead of running around in a blue funk trying to sort him out, I just left him to it. He had to iron his own unwashed shirt. When I got home after work he didn't even mention it. I don't suppose he'll rush to do it again, but it's a start. I must tell Bryony to try it with her kids.

Went to do a shoot at Pierre Vernaise's, the chef from Chez Domingo, *today. He lives in Knightsbridge. What a pile – he must be loaded. It was a bit embarrassing. His wife was there as we did the show, but he kept making passes at me. Kept whispering that I was the sexiest person he'd ever worked with – and in a French accent! For a minute I almost believed him. Nonsense of course, but hey, who's arguing. Jim was getting really jealous. He could hardly hold his clipboard steady.*

Jim's going to bring his daughter Jodie over on Sunday – that should be a clash of the Titans. I wonder how Matt will react. I don't really know what he thinks about girls, even pretty ones like Jodie. He never talks about any at school or comments on any of the girls on telly. Did see him looking slightly uncomfortable in the trouser department when Kylie was on, however, and there were some heavily torn-up pictures in his waste-paper bin that looked suspiciously like girls' bits. I reckon he downloads them from the Net. I should say something I suppose, but what? Tried to get him to cut the back lawn this evening, but he refused, saying it would harm all the creatures who lived in it. He really is the laziest, most unhelpful kid I've ever known.

Things Are Looking Up

Sunday 19th May

'Matt, are you in? What are you doing?'

'What do you want now?'

'Jim's arrived with Jodie. Could you come down?'

'I'm a bit busy.'

'Please, Matt, let's not have all that again.'

'Can't it wait?'

'Don't be so rude. Get down here right away, I won't ask you again. Sorry, Jodie. See, I'm apologising already and you haven't even met him. How are you? I haven't seen you for ages . . .

'Ah, there you are, Matt. Jodie, this is Matt. Matt, this is Jodie. You've already met Jim. '

'Er . . . hi.'

'Hi.'

'Jodie goes to that girls' school on the Bridgeford Road.'

'Oh – er – right.'

'Do you know the one?'

'No.'

'What's it like as a school, Jodie?'

'All depends, I suppose. I haven't been to any others.'

'Matt, darling, I thought you might want to show Jodie your computer, while I get lunch ready.'

'Why? Does she fix 'em or something?'

'Do you have to be so sarcastic? I expect she'll be interested, that's all. Do you like computers, Jodie?'

'I don't really like them or not like them. They're just what they are. I don't play stupid games on them or anything like that.'

'I think that must be a boy thing. Do you ever play computer games, Jim?'

'I used too, Packman and things, but they all got too complicated for me. I haven't got the patience.'

'Did you say Packman, Dad? Blimey, that must have been when computers were steam-powered.'

'OK, Little Miss Clever. Why don't you go up and have a look at Matt's computer?'

Matt's room

'Sorry about that. I just can't seem to talk in front of my ma.'

'Same here. I can never think of anything to say.'

'I'm even worse with my dad. Did you meet my sister Charlie?'

'Yeah, she was in the front garden talking to someone on her mobe. Is she the clever one?'

'You've heard. She never fails at anything and everyone thinks she's the dog's bollocks – oops, sorry.'

'Oh that's OK. It must drive you bonkers.'

'They already think I'm bonkers.'

'You seem fairly normal to me. Well, fairly.'

'I suppose it's because I never talk much.'

'You're talking now.'

'It's different. You're sort of . . . well . . . different.'

'What's your dad like? Do you get on with him?'

'Not really. I think he prefers Charlie.'

'The old father-daughter thing.'

'I don't know. It's weird. Nothing I ever do seems to please him. I've given up trying.'

'It might get better later.'

'I don't really care that much.'

'Actually, could you show me what you do on your computer. I am interested really. It's just that I hate to be treated like a kid. I've just got a laptop. Dad had a spare at work.'

'Tell me about it. I reckon parents are always about three years behind.'

'I don't really know if it's their fault. I suppose it must be difficult taking someone seriously when you've breast-fed them and changed their nappies.'

'I've never thought of that and I'd rather not if that's all right. I think my mum preferred me as a baby. She's a bit of a control freak, you see. Babies can't answer back.'

'I bet you did!'

'I bloody had to. It's called the survival of the fittest!'

From: 'Matt' <mattmason@coolmail.com>
Date: Sunday 19th May
To: hans@coolmail.com
Subject: Babe Alert! Babe Alert!

Christ, Hans, I can't believe it. You remember me telling you about that bloke Jim, the one who's been 'seeing' my ma. Well, he brought his daughter round to ours today. She's only just left, and I'm in LOVE with a capital Hard-On!!!! Talk about fit. I didn't think about it when Mum said this guy was bringing his daughter over . . . till I saw her. What a top of the pile, no questions asked, too-good-for-this-sad-world babe. Long blonde hair, long blonde legs, top-quality boobs, cool clothes — hell, man, she was so gorge I could hardly speak when I first saw her. And my mum and this Jim guy were practically begging her to come up to my room to play with me. Mad or what? Like asking a fox cub to play with a bunch of hounds. Asking for trouble I say (or not, as it turned out. I was too bloody nervous).

She's dead pretty, Hans, honest, and nice with it. Showed her what I do on the computer, graphics and stuff and some of the writing. She said she thought it was neat. I nearly said I thought she was neat, but chickened out. (Plonker!) Got to think of a way of seeing her again.

Any ideas?

Matt

Sunday 19th May

At last signs of life from Matt. Jim brought Jodie over today and he was completely smitten. When Jim suggested she went up to his room, I could tell he was trying to appear cool, but couldn't wait. They could hardly take their eyes off each other over lunch, but Matt seemed more tongue-tied than ever. He hardly ate a thing, poor lamb, and it WAS lamb – one of his favourites. Then, later, when I asked him what he thought of her, his exact words were, 'All right, I suppose', which for him is praise indeed. Then he asked me, as casually as he could manage, where Jim lived. Poor kid. He found it hard enough to ask the questions, let alone trying to appear uninterested in the answers. What's that all about? Perhaps it's just me and Charlie he has the problem with. He even seems to like Jim more *than us. Anyway, next Saturday night is **JIM NIGHT**. I've asked him to stay over. I'm as nervous as hell. Even Jim thinks it'll be a bit difficult. I'm seeing the girls for coffee on Saturday morning. Maybe they'll have some ideas.*

Got a call from that chef on Friday – Pierre what's-his-name . . . The one whose house we went to. He said he'd like to cook dinner for me at his restaurant. Christ, if my life isn't complicated enough without getting involved with a married man – and a famous married man at that – and a French, famous married man at that. Having said all that, I've never been to Chez Domingo *– too pricey by half. No harm in just having dinner, though, I suppose? What am I saying? Ah well, I can fantasise.*

New Sister

From: 'Matt' <mattmason@coolmail.com>
Date: Wednesday 22nd May
To: hans@coolmail.com
Subject: My New Sister

Hi. Just had a deeply dreadful thought. If Jodie's dad were to marry my ma, she'd be my sister or something hideous like that. That'd put a stop to my evil plans. I don't think you're allowed to bonk your sister in this country. I expect you can in Germany, being foreign and all.

Vat's all zis about zis girl Gretchen . . . the one at school? I need details, man. How old is she? Does she get the jokes? Is she babular? Does she snog? — you know the sort of thing.

Reply immediately or else,

Matt

'Matt darling, are you all right?'

'Uh!'

'You've hardly eaten a thing. I usually have to stop you licking the pattern off the plate.'

'I'm not hungry.'

'We know why that is, don't we, Mother.'

'All right, Charlie. That's enough. Don't pick on him.'

'What you getting at, Charlie?'

'Oh nothing.'

'You're making a hell of a lot of noise for someone saying nothing.'

'You can talk, Matt. You nev. . .'

'C'mon you two, let's have a break.'

'I'm sick of her taking the piss, Mum. She's never off my case. Just because I don't like cauliflower cheese, I get the third bloody degree.'

'You've never said you didn't like it when I made it before.'

'Maybe I'm too polite.'

'*You!* Too polite – I don't think so.'

'I bet he can't even spell it, Mum.'

'Look Charlie, one more word and you can have my cauliflower cheese . . . right in your stupid mush.'

'Stop it you two, for Christ's sake. I've had just about enough of all this arguing.'

'Why can't you leave me alone then, both of you. I

never start these things. Anyway, I've had enough too. I'm going to my room.'

'Not before you've taken Elvis for a walk.'

'Oh shit, do I have to do everything?'

'Look, he's your dog.'

'Why couldn't we have got a dog that walked itself?'

'Matt, walk your blasted dog NOW. That's not a request, it's an order.'

```
From: 'Matt' <mattmason@coolmail.com>
Date: Wednesday 22nd May
To: hans@coolmail.com
Subject: Murder at Randolph Drive
```

I need a ticket out of here before I break the place up. Charlie was trying to make out I couldn't eat cos of Jodie. Trouble is, she was probably right — the slagster. That made it a trillion times worserer.

As for Jodie, I just can't seem to get her out of my mind (just like the Kylie song). Blimey, I'm not even getting off on my wicked Kylie poster any more — seriouso or what? Jeez, hope this isn't what love's like. I can't do much at the best of times, but now I'm like the walking dead. It's like I'm trapped in one of those crappy boy-band songs.

Do you feel that way about this Gretchen girl you're seeing? You don't sound that bothered either way. Maybe that's a German thing.

Anyway, auf Wiedersehen for now (that's also German, you know), I'm off down the park with Elvis. Führer's orders.

See you,

Matt

Wednesday 22nd May

Unless I'm completely mistaken, poor Matt's completely besotted. I could have put a Big Mac and fries in front of him tonight, followed by chocolate-chip ice cream, and he wouldn't have looked at them. The agony and the ecstasy. Why is it only young people who feel so intensely? I love Jim to bits, but I can easily put him into another compartment while I get on with my life. When you're Matt's age it takes you over completely. Even so, I'm not sure girls get it quite so bad – probably because they seem to be able to offload on to their mates. If only Matt would speak to me or even his dad (not that he'd be much use). The poor kid's so locked in, he can hardly function. I wonder if he tells any of his mates or that friend in

44

Germany about it? I do hope so, otherwise he'll explode. I'd like to ask Jim if he can find out if Jodie feels the same, but I suppose it would be sticking my nose where it doesn't belong.

From: 'Matt' <mattmason@coolmail.com>
Date: Wednesday 22nd May
To: hans@coolmail.com
Subject: Lost Soul Alert

Sorry about the second e-mail. This Jodie thing's getting out of hand. At school today, I even stumbled into the wrong lesson. Jeez, Hans, I sat down in 15A with the Sixth Form. Funny or what. They all thought it was a hoot too, but Skinner made out I was taking the piss and sent me upstairs. I bet you miss old Skinhead — vat a vanker. Mrs Goldstein, the new Head Teacher, wasn't too bad actually. It was almost as if she'd seen that look before. Don't know how. She couldn't have ever been in the same sitch — not with a guy anyway.

I bet Jodie hasn't even thought about me since Sunday. There's me walking around like a total spaced-out dickhead, and she's probably out and about skipping around with her mates (who are probably all blokes).

It's so not cool all this. There's me, master of the universe, journalist extraordinaire, losing it over a flipping girl. God knows why I'm telling you all this. I suppose it's because I'd feel a bit prattish saying it out loud . . . and you're far enough away for it not to matter.

What's to become?

Matt

Was That Her Name?

'Mum, you know the girl who came at the weekend?'

'Do you mean Jodie, Jim's daughter?'

'Oh yeah, I think that was her name.'

'C'mon Matt, you know very well it was. What about her?'

'I – er – promised I'd find out something for her. I just wondered if you had her number.'

'That's nice. What did she want to know?'

'Oh – er – nothing much. It was just a website.'

'She lives with her mother, I'm afraid. I'll have to ask Jim when I see him.'

'When's that?'

'Well, I could ring Jim I suppose. There's no great hurry, is there?'

'No, not really. It's just that I sort of promised. So what are YOU laughing at, Charlie?'

'You fancy her rotten and you don't want to let on.'

'I wouldn't tell you if I did, you spasmo.'

'You do, don't you? It's so obvious.'

47

'Look, get off my back – why don't you? I wouldn't pry into your life, even if you had one.'

'I've got more of a life than you. I think you prefer computers to girls.'

'At least you can switch 'em off. That's more than you can with you.'

'She was very pretty, Matt.'

'Don't you start, Mum. Why can't you both leave me alone?'

'What's the big problem? Why shouldn't you fancy a pretty girl?'

'It's got nothing to do with you, or Charlie, that's why. I'm going upstairs.'

'To make love to your computer?'

'C'mon, Charlie, leave him alone.'


```
From: 'Matt' <mattmason@coolmail.com>
Date: Thursday 23rd May
To: hans@coolmail.com
Subject: Murder in the Suburbs
```

```
If you read about a double homicide in a
quiet suburban street just outside London,
it'll be Charlie and my mum. They're tak-
ing the piss out of me big time, because
of Jodie. That's the trouble — if I do say
anything, they jump down my throat, and if
```

I don't, they think I'm hiding something. Do you find that with your personal old people?

Anyway, after a whole bunch of interrogation, Mum promised to get her number (God knows what I'm going to say). Don't even know where she lives. Probably Outer Mongolia, knowing my luck. Shit and sugar — I'm so stupid — why didn't I get her e-mail address? That would be loads easier than talking. I think I've got sad brain syndrome with all this thinking about a bloody girl. Either that or I'm turning into one. Please feel free to take the piss. Got to get off to school now.

How's that Gretchen?

Reply soon . . .

Or else!

Matt

Thursday 23rd May

Time to empty the old guilt bag. I started thinking I had something on Matt. I worked out that if he wants to see Jodie again, he'll have to keep in with Jim – and me, come to that. Then I realised it was a bit like trying to score points off my own son – blackmail even.

Poor kid, I almost felt sorry for him today – almost. It cost him plenty to ask me a favour, even if it was just a telephone number. I bet when I get it, he'll make out he doesn't really care. What is it about boys of that age? So scared of showing any feelings whatsoever. I suppose Charlie and I were a little hard on him. It's just that he takes it all so seriously. I wonder if it's just a thing boys go through?

I know something's going on though. He brought down a whole load of empty cups this morning and his bedclothes for washing . . . and two plastic bags of rubbish. That must be some sort of a record. He's cleaning his room in case Jodie comes again. It's funny, sometimes I can't make him out at all and other times I can read him like a book.

With Jim staying over this Saturday, I'm now beginning to worry about Charlie. It's not that she's a prude or anything, but I'm not sure how she'll react to Jim and me sleeping under the same roof (let alone in the same bed). Up to now, since her father left, she's had me all to herself. Maybe I should have a word. Who'd have thought it would ever come to this – having to ask permission from my own teenage daughter to have nookie.

From: 'Matt' <mattmason@coolmail.com>
Date: Thursday 23rd May
To: hans@coolmail.com
Subject: Home Match

Thanks for getting back so soon and not thinking I'm soppy. It's really good to dump stuff on someone — even you! Feel free to do the same. I've been thinking about something else. Much as I can't get my head round the idea of my mum doing it with another bloke — any bloke — I suppose I'd better encourage this thing she's got with Jodie's dad if I want to keep seeing Jodie.

I now reckon my mum wants to do it with him on the premises, a sort of home match if you know what I mean. She keeps hinting about it. What a ghastly, sick-making thought — my mum at it in another room. I reckon she's too scared of what I'll say to come out with it. Still, I reckon I'd better keep my mouth shut, whatever happens. Sorry I've been going on. I dare say you Germans have problems of your own.

You said you snogged Gretchen in your last e-mail. What do Germans kiss like? Girls, I mean. Do they do tongues and stuff? I'd be a bit careful if I was you. One big snog and she'll want to take you over. You know what you lot were like with Poland! And keep an eye on your frankfurter — ha ha. Sorry about the German jokes, but we've just been doing the war in History. I bet they have a whole load about us. Let me know.

Keep on keeping on,

Matt

All Systems Go

'Ah Matt, there you are. I didn't know if you were in. I've got Jodie's number.'

'Oh, er . . . right.'

'So, when are you thinking of ringing her?'

'Uh?'

'I asked you when are you going to ring Jodie? I thought you wanted to.'

'When I get round to it. Why, what's it got to do with you?'

'No reason, I just thought it might be nice.'

'What might be nice?'

'If you two were friends.'

'Why?'

'Well, she could come over with Jim sometimes, and you could do things together.'

'You see, Mum, there you go again. Always trying to control stuff. If I want to ring her or see her, I'll do it. Is that, OK?'

'I was only trying to help. I thought you liked her.'

53

'She was all right, I suppose.'

'Only all right?'

'Oh! OK, more than all right. Now, are you satisfied? . . . Blimey!'

From: 'Matt' <mattmason@coolmail.com>
Date: Thursday 23rd May
To: hans@coolmail.com
Subject: Progress Report

Got Jodie's number off Mum. What a struggle that was. Like nicking a bone off a mad dog. Why can't she just do something and leave it? Anyway, that was the good news. The bad news is trying to think of what to say — I do crap phone . . . to girls that is (and dads). Trouble is, I know nothing about her. She's probably got a zillion blokes queuing up — all tall and older with cars and stuff. All I've got is a crap bike, an even crappier skateboard and the beginnings of a brand new spot. I think the only way to go is the humorous, arsy, don't—give-a-monkey's about any-thing route — I can't really compete on any other. Should I try to take her out? If so, where? She doesn't exactly look a park bench type, especially with a father like that. And with what? I'm suffering from the old nil dosho syndromo as per usual. Dad's supposed to give me some, but he always forgets, and I can't bear asking. Never really needed much cash, up till now — apart from for servicing my extreme crack and alcohol habits of course.

Christ, I might have to get a job or something (quickly washes mouth out with soap). The things I'm prepared to do for love (or lust?).

How's that Gretchen doing? She sounds brill — and more to the point — rich. You said her dad's got a Porsche, and her mum rides a BMW motorbike with a nose-ring (her mum, not the bike!). How bloody cool is that? Is it true you can drive at any speed you like on the motorways over there?

Is she a babe, this Gretchen? I don't really know what German girls look like. Tall and blonde, aren't they — with little black moustaches? (Sorry, there I go again!)

More information required, mein Herr,
Matt

Thursday 23rd May

Getting anything out of Matt is like reeling in a large awkward fish. Just as you think you might have him, he wriggles out of it. I can tell he really fancies Jodie, but will he admit it? If only I could find one thing that we could talk about, it might open up everything else.

I still have very little idea how he's doing at school. I suppose the only way to find out is to ring them. Trouble is, I'm scared of what I might hear. I think he might be doing some sort of magazine project or something. Found a whole load of paper when I was clearing out his bin. I shouldn't really have looked, but it's the only way of finding out what he's up to. If he wrote it, it's not bad at all. Quite political and grown up – and funny. Where does that come from? Maybe John. He was always a good writer – but I don't remember the funny bit, but that could be because of what happened. Again, I'd like to ask Matt about it, but I'm sure he'd deny everything or accuse me of prying.

I'm beginning to worry about Charlie. She's suddenly become very quiet and worried-looking. She generally rushes home from school to tell me everything and now she's gone silent. I hope it's not because of Jim and me. Perhaps something's gone wrong at school.

Now she just moons about the house, looking pre-

occupied and sad. Hope it's just a passing thing. With any luck she'll be as right as rain in a few days. Teenagers! Who'd have 'em? It's a bit like juggling with wet hands, especially when there's only one of you. Every time you think you've got the hang of it, you drop something and have to start again.

From: 'Matt' <mattmason@coolmail.com>
Date: Thursday 23rd May
To: hans@coolmail.com
Subject: Well-Received PANTS — Ha Ha!

Guess what? Forgot to tell you. Loads of people came back to me over the latest PANTS and really seemed to like it. What did you think? Have you got it yet? In the next one, I'm going to have a go at all the scrapping between the Israelis and the Palestinians. Daring or what? I hope I get it right.

What are German politics all about? I don't even know if you've got a president or a presidentess or a king or a queen. You could have our lot if you want. They're all German anyway from way back. I read that somewhere. I know you don't have an army, cos nobody'll let you have one

after what you did with your last one — ha
ha. Could you send me a bit about Germany
for the paper? Wouldn't that be cool?
PANTS's own foreign correspondent kind of
thing.

Still not missing you one bit.

Matt

Matt Braves the Phone

Friday 24th May

'Oh – er – hi there, is that Jodie?'

'Yeah, who's that?'

'It's Matt . . . Matt Mason. D'you remember me? You came round to our place last Sunday. Your dad's going out with my . . .'

'Course I do, silly. How are you? How did you get my numero?'

'My mum asked your dad. Do you mind?'

'Course not. It's really cool. I'll give you my mobe. How you doing?'

'Still alive – just. I just thought I'd ring . . . You're not busy, are you? If you are I could call another time . . .'

'No way. I've only got a bit of English lit. tonight. Then I'm going to try and sneak out without the Guardian of the Gate seeing.'

'Who's that?'

'Oh, just my mum. She's all right really, just a bit over-inquisitive.'

'Mine wrote the bloody book. Anyway, where d'you go when you escape?'

'Either down the park with my mates or round to Sacha's. She lives in the next road. Do you get much homework?'

'Sort of, but I can never seem to get into it. I read tons, but not what they want me to.'

'Same here. What are you into at the moment?'

'One of those Philip Pullman things.'

'Any good?'

'Beats Harry bloody Potter!'

'Matt, I wanted to ask you on Sunday . . . what do you make of your mum being with my dad?'

'I think it's a bit weird, if you want the absolute truth.'

'Why? Don't you like my dad?'

'Oh, he seems cool enough. I just can't work out what he's doing with my mum.'

'What do you mean? Whether they do it and stuff?'

'No, not that. Christ, I haven't got that far. I don't really want to think about that. No, he seems all kind of sorted out, cool-looking with a flash car, great job and all that, and he's going after my mum. It just seems a bit odd.'

'I think she's really neat. Fit even.'

'Who, my mum?'

'Yeah, I wouldn't mind looking like that when I'm her age.'

'Blimey, I suppose I've never really thought about it. I

suppose when I look at my mates' mums she's not too bad . . .'

'Anyway, it can't be all bad. If my dad hadn't met your mum, I'd never have met you.'

'Whah? Blimey.'

'Anyway, I think she's really nice, and that's the main thing.'

'You don't have to live with her. Talk about a control freak.'

'She can't be that terrible. Does your sister get on with her?'

'Oh yeah, not much! Everyone loves Charlie and Charlie loves everyone.'

'Aren't you an incy-wincy bit jealous?'

'Of her? No flipping fear.'

'Look, I've been wondering if we could meet again. Maybe you could come over here or something? I was going to call you.'

'Really?'

'Really.'

'I don't even know where you live. I thought at first you lived with your dad.'

'No, Mum and me live in Rainsdon Park Road – about five miles away. You must know it.'

'I could cycle that far.'

'Well, why don't you then?'

'Well, I will then.'

'Well, do then.'

'Well, OK then – when then?'

'How's about tomorrow? I'll be in all day, and Mum and Brian won't.'

'Who's Brian?'

'Her new man.'

'What's he like?'

'A bit of a Norman Normal, but fairly harmless.'

'Jeeeeeesus, they're all at it, these oldsters.'


```
From: 'Matt' <mattmason@coolmail.com>
Date: Friday 24th May
To: hans@coolmail.com
Subject: Stop Press
```

What do you make of this? I rang that wicked Jodie babe and she said she thought that her dad and my mum getting together wasn't all bad, because it meant she'd got to meet me. Whoah, steady!!!!!!! Hey, is that awesome or what? And she really does hang around parks — she told me. Anyway, you know I said I needed some money quick. Well I now need it quicker. Got any spare Euros kicking around you don't need? I hear the streets are paved with them out there. She's asked me over to her place tomorrow, so I haven't got long. I suppose you have to buy a ticket to win the lottery, don't you?

Glad to hear you've got a newspaper going in your school too. Perhaps I could be the English correspondent. Cool, eh? Hey, wouldn't it be wicked to have a network of underground student newspapers throughout the world. Students unite, sort of thing. It could be brilliant. We could have kids from the Middle East, Russia — even Iraq — e-mailing us anonymously. How cool would that make us? What do you think?

Over to you,

Matt

Friday 24th May

Jim says he rang his wife and Jodie's been asking all about my Matt. Now I'm beginning to worry about how he's going to treat her. Honestly, if I didn't have something to worry about, I'd worry about having nothing to worry about. Anyway, if he treats her like he does me and Charlie, it'll be all over before it begins. Luckily, no one else in their right mind would put up with it.

Mind you, if he gets a girlfriend, it might make him

get his act together. Then again, it might not. If Jim's right, Jodie sounds not much better than him. Why can't his father ever deal with these things?

Feeling rather pleased with myself. Decided not to go to Pierre's restaurant this evening. He wasn't at all pleased, but as soon as I told him, I knew I'd done the right thing. What is it about married men – well, French married men? It's as if they think that every single woman over thirty's desperate. And how did he know I was divorced? I never told him. Is it that obvious? Is there some sort of needy expression on my face? Anyway, I told him that I'm seeing someone and that even if I wasn't, he's married and I don't go there.

Don't know whether Matt's phoned Jodie. These kids are more secretive than us – and that's saying something. Had yet another ruck with him today. Just because I asked him not to eat with his face two inches from the plate. I wonder sometimes if I'm being too controlling, but if I don't teach him, or the school don't either, who will? Certainly not his father.

From: 'Matt' <mattmason@coolmail.com>
Date: Friday 24th May
To: hans@coolmail.com
Subject: Up the Tories!

What do you make of this? I saw this ad in the local paper — leafleting for the Conservative Party. Worry not, I haven't gone over to the enemy, I just need dosh — their dosh. It's great, man. I'll be like the spy within — ha ha . . . Robin Hood, robbing the rich to pay the poor (that's me — if you were wondering).

PANTS is pretty awesome. People are asking when the next one's out. I'm still working on the Middle East business (any chance of your bit?) and I'm hoping to get it in the next issue.

Sorry to hear you broke up with Gretchen. Bloody Germans, eh! You said she reckoned you were too immature. We could show her who's mature or not, couldn't we — NOT! Hope you're not too heartbroken. Plenty more Fräuleins in the sea (and fish). Also, sorry to hear that they're shoving speed limits on more and more motorways over there. How annoying is that? By the time you get your licence it'll be the same as the UK. We'll all be driving bloody milk floats.

Take care,

Matt

65

To Jodie's and Beyond

Saturday, 25th May: morning

'Mum, have you seen my Simpsons T-shirt.'

'Isn't it in the pile that's just been ironed?'

'Whah?'

'If it isn't there, it hasn't been washed. Sorry, sweetheart.'

'But I need it today, I'm going out.'

'You've got millions of T-shirts.'

'Yeah, but I need that one.'

'Why, where are you off to?'

'Nowhere special.'

'So why do you have to *wear* something special? Are you back for lunch?'

'No.'

'Don't forget to take your mobile. Where *are* you actually going, Matt? I'm only interested.'

'Oh Christ, Mum, if you *actually* can't live without knowing, I'm going over to Jodie's. Oh, and here comes big sister Charlie to put her oar in.'

'I thought I heard you say you're going to see Jodie.

See! I knew you fancied her.'

'Leave him alone, Charlie.'

'Yeah, there's a good girl – leave me alone. Go play on the motorway.'

'So what's so wrong about being good? Anyway, you haven't a clue what I get up to.'

'And I don't bloody want to. You could shag a whole football team for all I care.'

'Matt! I don't like you talking like that.'

'Anyway, who says I haven't?'

'*You*, Charlie? You wouldn't know where to start.'

'David Beckham wouldn't be bad.'

'You're so bloody tabloid.'

'So when did you become so above it all? Lord Mason of Randolph Drive, is it?'

'Sounds better than Charlie Beckham.'

'OK, that's enough, you two. Let me know when you're on your way back, Matt.'

'Would *never* be all right?'

From: 'Matt' <mattmason@coolmail.com>
Date: Saturday 25th May
To: hans@coolmail.com
Subject: Big Day Out

Had to tell the two witches of Randolph Drive where I was going today. It's got to the point where it's easier to own up than to keep anything from them. Mum just has to know everything I do. It really pisses me off.

Biked over to Jodie's place. She's so cool — not really like a girl . . . or not like any of the girls I've ever known. You'd have loved it. She introduced me to all her mates — girl mates. Spoiled for choice I was. All really fit apart from one. They even bought me a Big Mac, as I still haven't got any dosh. That's so cool it slides off the thermometer.

Take it easy,

Matt

Saturday, 25th May

Matt came home in a dream today. What a turn-up! I fall for Jim and Matt falls for his daughter. Pity he doesn't have a son for Charlie. Charlie's very weird at the moment. She seems to have lost interest in just about everything. She's not herself at all. I hope we're not in for a Matt II in the house. That would be grounds for suicide (or double murder).

Just got a letter from Matt's school. Apart from telling me how badly he's doing in his ordinary work, his form master went on about this newspaper thing he's involved with. He said it's very political and very controversial. Stranger still, he said, Matt's writing showed – what were his words? . . . 'A genuine commitment and an enthusiasm that was severely absent from his school work.' Just shows how much one knows one's own kids. Told John about it and he said he'd been very political when he was young. Christ knows where all his ideals went, he sure shows no signs of them now.

Tonight's the night for Jim's big sleep-over. I'll be interested to see who says what at breakfast. Dreading it. I'm going to talk to Matt as soon as I get a chance.

From: 'Matt' <mattmason@coolmail.com>
Date: Saturday 25th May
To: hans@coolmail.com
Subject: Delivery Boy

Started doing the leaflets for the Conservatives last night. Blimey, you need danger-money in some parts of town. Spent more time explaining that it was only a job and that I wasn't anything to do with them, than I did delivering the bloody things. Then one old geezer on that posh estate by the park said that he thought it was wonderful that young people like me were getting involved with the party and offered me a beer. Can't see what all the fuss is about, me. Labour's almost as right wing as the other lot anyway, but a beer's a beer.

What's this about having another girlfriend. Blimey, Hans, you don't hang about. I reckon you're conquering ze old Fatherland single-handed. Do they grow on trees out there? I mean — it can't be your charm or your looks. So who's this flipping Steffi when she's at home? Hope she's a bit prettier than that German tennis player called Steffi with the big hooter. The one who knocks around with Andre Agassi.

Still waiting for your big piece on Germany, by the way. By another way, since Jodie's come along, England's not looking quite so bad.

Keep up ze good work, mein Capitain
Matt

Rumblings at School

Sunday 26th May

'Mum, have you seen my jeans?'

'I was going to ditch them, they're completely worn out.'

'You whah? Are you some sort of crazy person?'

'The knees are right through and the bottoms are completely ragged. I've seen tramps dressed better.'

'So? That's the way I like them. Where are they now?'

'They're out in the laundry room, if you must know. On the floor by the washing machine.'

'Oh no, you haven't gone and washed them, have you?'

'Are you mad, I wouldn't put them in with any of our stuff – we might catch something. By the way, don't go away, I need to talk to you.'

'Uh?'

'I had a letter from your form master.'

'Oh no.'

'Oh *yes*! He's not very pleased with your work.'

'That makes two of us.'

'No Matt, that makes three of us, and if your dad hears, that'll make four of us. He says he knows for sure you've got it in you, but you don't try. He says that unless you pull your socks up you'll have real problems when you get to your GCSEs.'

'Is that why he wrote?'

'Well yes, but not only that. He says that some of the stuff you've been writing in that paper of yours could get you into serious trouble. He said he wanted to talk to me before he speaks to you.'

'How did he get to see it? It was never meant for grown-ups, let alone teachers.'

'It said in the letter he found a copy under one of the desks.'

'Oh fu . . . er – flip. I bet that was Dean, he's so bloody careless.'

'Mind you, he also said your writing showed real talent and that it was a shame that you never do any work of that quality in class.'

'Really?'

'Really.'

'It's only because I'm not interested in school stuff.'

'Could I read it, Matt?'

'What?'

'Your paper. I'd quite like to make up my own opinion.'

'You wouldn't like it either.'

'Why not? Try me.'

'You'll stop me doing it – I know you will. It's what you do.'

'Not necessarily. I might even fight your corner if I think it's good.'

'Really?'

'Really.'

'Blimey.'

```
From: 'Matt' <mattmason@coolmail.com>
Date: Sunday 26th May
To: hans@coolmail.com
Subject: Fan Hit by Shit!
```

Looks like I might have to come to Krautland after all. Everything's gone belly up over here. Ma got a letter from old man Phillips. He'd got hold of a copy of PANTS — True! Apparently he read her the riot act. He said if it got into the wrong hands I could be in deep, deep shitenhausen. I'd love to know which issue he's on about. I wonder if it was the one with the article on the royal family being a waste of oxygen? Or it could have been when I accused our Tony B. of having an affair with Wee Georgie

Bush. Oh no, I've just remembered. I also said that schoolteachers were only schoolteachers because they were too thick to be anything else . . . I bet that was it. He just might not have liked that. Dean did a cartoon of a teacher in his garden trying to work out which end of a spade you dig with. Oh no!

The other thing old Phillips said — and wait for this — was that despite everything, I showed real talent as a writer. Mum was a bit gobsmacked — almost as much as me.

And you, I suspect.

Hope all's well,

Matt

Sunday 26th May

Just read two of Matt's articles in his paper – one about teachers and the other about the royals. Where does he get all that stuff from? He never gives the impression of taking anything in, let alone having an opinion. He must be getting it off the internet. Trouble is, though I don't agree with him that much, he makes a lot of good points in a clear, well-informed way – and funny too. His bit about the royals I found myself almost agreeing with. He wrote that they walk around with their heads up their backsides the whole time, not having any idea how normal people live. He said that in his view they're the last gasp of a system well past its sell-by date, and that they perpetuate privilege and the class system. Not bad. Trouble is, he always goes too far. He said that we should do what they did in the olden days and put their heads on spikes and display them on Tower Bridge. I see where he's coming from, but like most anti-royalists, he doesn't come up with anything better. But that's nothing. His piece about teachers could have him hung from the school clock tower, never mind the royal family. Thank God there was nothing specific about Mr Phillips.

Anyway, it all seemed to go off all right last night when Jim stayed. If anything Charlie was more tight-lipped than Matt over breakfast. She really is odd these days. There's definitely something going on. It's as if there's something constantly on her mind. She hardly mentions school . . . or boys! I talked with John about it, but she's said nothing to him either.

From: 'Matt' <mattmason@coolmail.com>
Date: Sunday 26th May
To: hans@coolmail.com
Subject: Girls

How's Steffi? You didn't say. Is she babular? I bet she is. Girls, eh. Don't they drive you nuts. Blimey, Hans, what if I'm in love — how pants would that be? I tell you it ain't nice. I reckon it's giving me a stomachache — worse even. Mind you, that might be something to do with not eating. Thought I'd feel really cool, but I so don't. Is it normal to keep imagining her with other guys — laughing and snogging and stuff and not thinking about me at all?

Do you reckon I should tell her or keep schtum? Have you ever told a member of the other species you really fancy them? It has to rank pretty low on the old cool-o-graph, think you not?

That bloke Jim stayed over with my mum last night. It was dead peculiar lying in bed and thinking of them at it — not nice at all. Every time I heard a creak, I thought it was them, and when Elvis (our dog) started scratching and bumping his leg on the floor . . .! Still, I suppose I'd better keep my mouth shut if I want to keep seeing Jodie.

I wonder when old Phillips is going to tackle me about PANTS?

Anyway, love to the Germans!

Matt

More Questions

Monday 27th May

'Matt, before you go up, I've been meaning to ask. How did it go with Jodie on Saturday?'

'OK.'

'What did you do?'

'Nothing much.'

'Like what?'

'We just sat and talked if you must know. Then she took me out to meet her mates.'

'I hope you weren't too rude.'

'No way. Anyway she gives as good as she gets.'

'Well, don't rush it.'

'Oh, don't start, Mum, for God's sake.'

'You haven't even said if you like her.'

'She's all right.'

'Just all right?'

'Well, all right – very all right.'

'By the way, when are you going to do something about the state of your room?'

'I'll do it soon.'

'When?'

'When I do it, OK.'

'It's disgraceful, living like that.'

'Look, there's millions of people starving in the world and half the people in Africa are dying of AIDS. I hardly think the state of my room ranks up with all that.'

'They haven't got any choice.'

'Well, that's why I'm so lucky then . . . I have.'


```
From: 'Matt' <mattmason@coolmail.com>
Date: Monday 27th May
To: hans@coolmail.com
Subject: Jodie
```

I can't believe it. Just talked to my mum and we almost didn't end up fighting. Well almost — we fell at the last fence. She was asking about Jodie as usual, and for some weird reason, I nearly told her. I didn't, of course, but I sort of wanted to. What's that all about? It was as if I was after her approval sort of thing. Can't think why. Am I going soft? Next I'll be having to treat the old thing as a human being. It's all too much of a shock. Have you ever spoken to your parents about anything?

Matt

Monday 27th May

Well, well, well! Almost got something out of Matt today. I really don't get that boy. What a mess he's in. He sometimes seems almost desperate to talk, but also desperate not to let his guard down. Even so, it will be so good for him to have someone to care about more than himself. I noticed he hasn't worn those disgusting old jeans for the last couple of days and that he'd been trying to use my razor. Life's so much easier in the house. Almost too easy for comfort. Can't help feeling it's the calm before the storm.

From: 'Matt' <mattmason@coolmail.com>
Date: Monday 27th May
To: hans@coolmail.com
Subject: Families

Thanks for the return e-mail. Could hardly believe that you actually talk to your mum about stuff . . . and your sister. That's a world record. Is that common over your way? What a strange lot you are, to be sure. It never occurs to me to talk to my two, especially Charlie. She'd just carry on taking the mick. As for my dad, I wouldn't know where to start. He makes all the right noises about being interested, but somehow I don't believe him. If he'd really cared, he wouldn't have pissed off in the first place, would he.

Waiting for the poo to hit the fan at school. Phillips looked at me today like a tiger eyeing a sick antelope. Reckon he was waiting for exactly the right moment to pounce and rip my head off. I wonder what being expelled really feels like. Not that it really matters, I'm probably going to die from malnutrition anyway. I still can't get that Jodie out of my brain. It's driving me crazy. I just want to know if she feels the same.

Sorry to be such a sissy.

Will try harder,

Matt

By the way, do you remember that horrible bossy prefect Jamie Coulson from the Sixth Form, the one who kept giving us all that grief. Guess what? He joined the police. Now who'd ever have thought that?

Telephone Alert!

'Hello, is Matt there? It's Jodie.'

'Oh, hi Jodie – it's Matt's mum, Sandie. I'll just shout upstairs for him. Hang on.'

'Matt, darling, are you there?'

'Whah?'

'It's Jodie on the phone.'

'Whah?'

'It's Jodie.'

'Blimey! Oh – er – right! – Coming.'

'Here he is, Jodie.'

'Hello!'

'Hi Matt. I just thought I'd phone to say what a good time I had on Saturday. My friends thought you were really cool.'

'Jeez, they ought to get out more.'

'You're so stupid. You really don't think much of yourself, do you?'

'There you go. See, even you think I'm stupid.'

'Don't be daft, I think you're really funny.'

'OK, so I'm daft now – not stupid. I suppose that's an improvement.'

'No, I don't think that – and nor do you.'

'It's just a question of convincing everyone else.'

'Well you've convinced me. Anyway, what's been happening?'

'Oh much of the same. I'm in even deeper poo at school, apparently, according to Mum. I wrote these things in my paper *PANTS* and my form master found a copy. He's going to have it out with me, probably tomorrow.'

'I didn't know you wore paper pants.'

'Ha very ha.'

'Sorry, were they funny?'

'Supposed to be. But more often my jokes seem to get taken the wrong way.'

'Join the club. Hey, I wanted to say, I've been thinking about you a lot.'

'Flipping hell, have you?'

'Yeah, I was wondering when I can see you again. It's been three days.'

'Three days and three hours . . . and – er – about three and a half minutes. Whenever you like. How's about this weekend? I've been thinking about you too. It's all a bit weird.'

'Why?'

'I don't know. I don't think I've ever really liked a girl before, sort of properly. I've fancied them and stuff –

you know – but not really liked them.'

'Don't you fancy me then? Do you only *like* me?'

'Oh hell, I'm really crap at this. I get so embarrassed.'

'Well, do you?'

'What! – get embarrassed?'

'No – fancy me?'

'C'mon, give me a break.'

'Sometimes people need to be told.'

'OK, I'm telling you. I just can't stop thinking about you. I try to imagine your face, but I can't quite get it right. Look, I was wondering if I could have a photo?'

'I could send one over now on the e-mail as an attachment if you want. Clothed or unclothed?'

'Well, I – er . . .'

'Only joking. See, you don't get my jokes either sometimes. Could I have one of you?'

'Me . . . why?'

'Because I want one, stupid.'

'See, you called me stupid again.'

'Sorry Matt, I don't mean it, honest.'

'Anyway, talking about photos. I've only really got a recent one of me and it's at my Uncle Derek's wedding and I'm all dressed up. I can't send that.'

'You must.'

'Why must I?'

'Because I've asked you to. Mind you, I can't imagine you smart.'

'Don't go there. It frightens small animals.'

From: 'Matt' <mattmason@coolmail.com>
Date: Tuesday 28th May
To: hans@coolmail.com
Subject: Wow!

Dear Herr Camarade,
You're not going to believe this, but I think I've nearly got a girlfriend — me — a nearly girlfriend! Can'st thou believe it?

Jodie rang half an hour ago and told me that she's been thinking about me and wants a photo and stuff. I'm such a weirdo. I felt brilliant at first, like it was just about everything I ever wanted to hear, but now it's all going pear-shaped again. I'm such a prat. All I've ended up feeling is that she doesn't really know what I'm like and that when she eventually does, she'll run a mile. Girls like her just don't go out with blokes like me.

It's dead odd. I know I'm funny and all that, and I know I'm not ugly (well, not THAT ugly), and I know that I'm actually cleverer than a lot of the thickos at school that pass exams, but I know bugger-all about girls, apart from my horrible sister, especially good-looking, cool ones. I've only snogged a few and they were the pits. You remember Tessa Griggs in Year Ten — she was about the best, can you believe, but she used to get all hot and worked up, which made me panic a bit. She had a mouth like one of those things you unblock sinks with, you remember?

Have you got any tips — monster to monster sort of thing? I suppose you're having to work out how to pull in German again which must be twice as hard — or is it? When do you try to kiss them, zat's vat I vant to know. I'm really panicked that I'll blow it if I move in too quick on Jodie or blow it if I don't.

Please advise,

Matt

Tuesday 28th May

Feel terribly guilty for doing it, but I listened in on Matt's phone call, through the kitchen door. I think he thought I was watching EastEnders. *Couldn't believe what I was hearing. My little boy sounding so grown up and SO BLOODY NICE! Why can't he be like that with us, for Christ's sake? He obviously fancies Jodie like mad and she him. Hated the bit where he said he thought everyone thought he was stupid. I must have a word with Charlie about that. Trouble is, I never know whether he's joking or not. Most of the time he seems not to give a damn. There could be a lot about Matt I don't know.*

Suppose I'd better have another word about this newspaper business. It's tricky. I don't want to put him off something he's passionate about, but he could get into really serious trouble – and not just at school. I reckon if some of that stuff got into a local paper, it could run on to the tabloids, and then we could be dealing with libel suits. Can just see the headline – Local School in Anarchy Scandal: Is This What We're Teaching Our Children? *I'd better talk to him tomorrow.*

Legal Affairs

Wednesday 29th May

'Matt, where are you? I need to talk to you.'

'Uh?'

'I said I need to talk to you. Did you speak to Mr Phillips today?'

'I'm in the loo.'

'Please come down, Matt. I'm wearing my voice out . . .'

'Rest it then.'

'Don't be so rude . . . Ah, there you are. Have you spoken to Mr Phillips yet?'

'Yeah, during break.'

'Was he angry?'

'Not particularly. He just lectured me, as usual.'

'Was it fair?'

'Depends. I just told him I thought we lived in a free country where we could think what we want.'

'What did he say?'

'He said you could think it, but you couldn't say it – let alone write it. He said some of my stuff was libellous.

88

Especially the bit about the royal family.'

'Are you surprised?'

'C'mon, nobody takes them seriously.'

'That's just your opinion.'

'Anyway, he droned on about there being better ways of saying it that'd get me into less trouble. Then I told him that I reckoned the best way to punch a point home is to make it funny.'

'Did he agree?'

'Sort of. He asked if he could take a look at what I plan to put in the mag in future.'

'And?'

'And I said I'd think about it. I said I thought it was only libel if it was published and paid for. *PANTS* is just a give-away.'

'You might have a point. I could check at work if you like. In telly, we've got lawyers who have to check every time we breathe.'

'Would you, Mum?'

'Of course, we can't have you going to jail. What would Jodie do?'

'What do you mean?'

'I think she'd pine away.'

'Oh shut up, Ma. You're taking the piss again.'

From: 'Matt' <mattmason@coolmail.com>
Date: Wednesday 29th May
To: hans@coolmail.com
Subject: Thanks!

Hi Hans,
Had another almost OK talk with Ma today.
Two in a row — eh. She said she's going to
find out whether I can be done for the
stuff in PANTS. By the way, your bit on
Germany is great — it was dead funny. I
really liked those jokes about the
British, especially the one about Tony
Blair. Where did they come from?

Jodie sent her photo over last night.
I'm adding it to this e-mail. What d'you
think? Pretty bloody good work, eh? She's
even better than that in real life — she's
a better colour for a start. What does
Steffi look like? Got any pics? I bet you
a quid mine's better looking. We should
have a contest. It'd be like England v
Germany sort of thing all over again.

Things are definitely looking up,
Matt

Wednesday 29th May

Talked with Matt again today. More than one-word answers again. It's all getting too much. For once he listened to what I had to say and didn't go off on one. We were talking about the things he writes. I think he might be surprised at what our lawyer said. It's all right for people like Private Eye, *he said – they can afford to pay libel claims, but not Matt and his school mates. It might be Matt's first dose of the real world.*

There's definitely something up with Charlie. She seems really unhappy and preoccupied. What could it be? You hear so many stories about girls being bullied at school. It could be because she's so popular and successful. She won't talk to me though – she makes out everything's fine. That sort of thing really gets up the noses of the rough kids. Maybe I could ask Matt, while he's not completely hating me.

Worried Mummy

Thursday 30th May: *breakfast*

'Ah Matt, before you head off, could we talk?'

'Uh.'

'I just wanted to ask you about your sister.'

'What about her?'

'Have you noticed anything odd lately?'

'What's odder than usual? I don't know, I suppose she hasn't been talking at me so much. Thank the Lord for that – I say.'

'Do you think anything could be wrong at school?'

'Search me. I'm way too far down the feeding chain for her to tell me anything.'

'Do you think you could find out?'

'Shouldn't think so.'

'Would you try?'

'Look, why should I? She's never done anything for me.'

'Please, Matt.'

'No way. Look, Mum, it's nothing to do with me, whatever it is.'

'I might have guessed you'd be like that. By the way, I

asked our lawyer guy about the stuff you wrote. He said he thought it was quite funny but potentially dangerous. He said that he doubted whether anyone would come after you boys – there'd be no point – but they could really give the staff and governors of the school a really hard time for putting out stuff like that.'

'I'll go up and churn out some more then.'

'That's not actually very fair, Matt.'

'Fair? What's fair, for God's sake. What's so fair about making school so boring and making me go to it? What's so fair about getting into trouble for saying what you really think? Don't give me bloody fair.'

'Calm down. Didn't you say Mr Phillips offered to vet your stuff?'

'Only if I let him.'

'I think it might be a good idea. Now they know you exist, you could be hauled in at any time. You should keep the really strong stuff to yourself.'

'I might have guessed you'd say that.'

'And what do you mean by that?'

'You lot always go for the soft option.'

'Who's "you lot"? Oh Matt, you've got such a lot to learn.'

'You always say that too.'

'I used to be like you, until I realised there are different ways of doing things.'

'Yeah, like keeping your mouth shut and letting all the crap run over you.'

'It's called growing up, Matt.'

'OK, if that's the case, count me out.'

From: 'Matt' <mattmason@coolmail.com>

Date: Thursday 30th May

To: hans@coolmail.com

Subject: Trouble With Charlie

Quick e-mail before supper. Mum's worried about Charlie because she's been acting all weird and stuff (so what's new?). I asked around school a bit. Shit, man, I almost wished I hadn't. Lucy Carter, remember her? (Buck teeth and big boobs.) Well, she said she'd seen her snogging Shane Goodall behind the gym. SHANE GOODALL!!! I didn't believe her at first, but then I asked a couple of her mates and they swore it was true. Can you imagine anything remotely more crap than that? He's such a plonker — always going on about all the girls he's had. I just hope my sister's not one of them. What the hell do I do? I can't tell Mum. She thinks the sun shines out of Charlie's cute little backside. Trouble is, she is my sister, and I don't want people sniggering behind her back (let alone mine). I suppose I'd better have it out with Charlie, head-on? Or should I corner that tosser Goodall and risk having my head turned round 180 degrees?

  All ideas gratefully received,

  Matt

Thursday 30th May

Shock horror. Jim asked me to marry him today, silly man. I told him he was mad, but he said he loves me and he's never been more sure of anything (they all say that). I reckon he noticed the looks that bloody chef was giving me. Bet that's what brought all this on . . . he feels threatened. It's out of the question of course. I swore blind I'd never marry anyone again after John. Live with someone maybe, but I'm not going through all that nonsense again. I know! I could ask Jodie to be a bridesmaid alongside Matt as a page-boy. I'm sure he'd really love that.

* This girlfriend business seems to have really knocked Matt for six. It certainly takes the heat off me. There's no doubt that having a bright, pretty girl fancying him has given him the sense of self-worth that he's been looking for. Christ, I sound like a shrink, or a bloody agony aunt. I just hope that if*

it all goes wrong, which it almost certainly will, he won't climb right back into his lead-lined shell. Watch this space.

What a Charlie!

'Hey Charlie, can I come in? It's Matt.'

'Hang on a minute. Look, I'm busy. What do you want?'

'I gotta talk to you, it's important.'

'Oh all right, if you have to.'

'Christ, Charlie, what a bloody mess. Your room's usually like Barbie's bathroom.'

'If that's what you wanted to tell me, then you can just –'

'No, just a bit shocked, that's all. It's almost as bad as mine.'

'I've had quite a lot going on lately. I haven't had time.'

'Yeah – I think I know why.'

'What do you mean – you know why? You don't know what's going on in my life.'

'Tell me then.'

'Tell you what?'

'It's something at school, isn't it?'

'Like what?'

'You've got involved with a bloke.'

'What bloke? What do you mean? What are you getting at?'

'I think I know what's going on, Charlie.'

'OK, Mr Clever Clogs. You tell me.'

'I know who you've been knocking around with.'

'So, who's that?'

'Do I have to say the prick's name?'

'How bloody dare you. Get out of here!'

'You've been seeing Shane Goodall, haven't you?'

'What if I have? What's it got to do with you?'

'Nothing at all, but you've been all weird lately. More weird than usual. Still, if you don't want to talk about it.'

'It's nobody's bloody business but mine.'

'Hey, you're crying. Are you all right, Charlie?'

'Please leave me alone, Matt. Please.'

```
From: 'Matt' <mattmason@coolmail.com>
Date: Friday 31st May
To: hans@coolmail.com
Subject: The Plot Thickens
```

This business with Charlie's worse than I thought. Tried to get what was going on but she clammed up and then started blubbing. Since then I've been doing a bit

more detective work. Her best friend,
Daisy, told me the lot and seemed glad to
do it. It's all about that Goodall prat.
She's been trying to ditch him,
apparently, but he won't have any of it —
at least till he's had her. I think she's
like a kind of trophy — Head Girl and all.
I'm not sure what to do. I think I'm going
to have to go back and tackle her again.
This could be really serious.

Hope you're OK,
Matt

Charlie's room – later

'Charlie, are you in there? It's me again. I need to talk a
bit more.'

'Go away, Matt. I told you, it's nothing to do with
you.'

'Look, I'm coming in anyway.'

'Oh shit, Matt. What is it this time?'

'I know exactly what's going on. I'm going to stay
here till you tell me about it.'

'Who've you been talking to?'

'Daisy. She seemed really worried about you and
Goodall.'

'She had no right to talk to you.'

'She said she didn't care. She said that's what mates are for. Now come on, what's going on?'

'OK, if you must know, I have been sort of seeing Shane.'

'Why?'

'I don't know why. I suppose I must have fancied him. I've been getting so fed up with everyone calling me a goody-goody and he seemed sort of dangerous.'

'I thought you really got off on the good-girl thing.'

'It's like a game – I do it almost to see how far I can go.'

'But Head Girl and everything, and wanting to help people and everything – jeez!'

'I suppose I just want everyone to like me.'

'What? Like *any* people?'

'I just really want everyone's approval.'

'Blimey, you must tell me about it. So what about this Goodall cretin? How long's it been going on?'

'A couple of months, I suppose.'

'Do you still fancy him?'

'No way. You're right, he's a pig – and that's unfair to pigs. I hate him.'

'So why are you still seeing him?'

'He won't let me go, Matt, honest. He keeps saying he'll do something if I try to pack him up. I think he doesn't want to lose face in front of his mates.'

'Have you actually done it with him?'

'No, I haven't! Honest, Matt, you must believe me.

That's the trouble. He keeps trying, but I won't let him. It was when I said I wouldn't go there the last time, he threatened me. He said I'd been leading him on, but I hadn't, honest. I don't know what to do. I'm so scared he might actually force me.'

'How? What's he threatening to do?'

'He say's he'll go to the police.'

'Why, because you won't do it?'

'No, course not. I stole something from a club – a mobile. He forced me to do that too. It was like a dare. Look, there's a lot you don't know about me. I'm not quite the sweet little thing you think I am.'

'Compared to me you are.'

'I bet you didn't even know I've had my belly button pierced.'

'Whah? Does Mum know?'

'Course not. It's all part of the game.'

'Back to Goodall going to the law. That's a bloody laugh. He's got more reason than just about anyone to avoid 'em.'

'I don't know what to do, Matt.'

'You should probably tell Mum or Dad.'

'Oh God, no. Please don't tell them, Matt. Please. Promise me you won't. Can't you just leave it. I'll sort it out.'

'What if you can't?'

'Look, why are you so interested?'

'Because you're my sister. He can be a vicious bastard.'

'Please leave it alone. Please, Matt.

From: 'Matt' <mattmason@coolmail.com>
Date: Friday 31st May
To: hans@coolmail.com
Subject: Shane Goodall

The crap has strucken ze fan, mein Camarade — well and bloody truly. I was right, that bastard Goodall's threatening my sister because she won't let him do what he wants to her. I suppose I've got to do something, but I can't think what. If you'd ever seen what he did to that bloke from Sheldon High, you'd understand my problem. Did you hear about it?

Spoke to Jodie about it tonight. She got all protective. I felt great, for a while, all sort of heroic and everything. Unfortunately, as you well know — heroic I actually ain't, but she doesn't know that . . . yet!

What the hell do I do?

Matt

Friday 31st May

Now I know it – something's definitely going on. I talked to Matt again and he was really abrupt. Said he didn't know anything. He said Charlie wouldn't tell him anything anyway. He was lying, I could tell. I just know she's in trouble – it's a mother thing. It's odd, but I think it's something quite serious. It's almost like a payment for being so perfect all these years. I even rang John last night and he sounded really concerned for once. He couldn't bear anything to happen to his precious little girl. I only wish he felt that way about Matt.

If all this isn't enough, Jim started pressing me today about us all moving in with him. I gave him a flat no, and said that I'd only think about it when the time was right. I told him I thought Charlie was in some sort of trouble and that I couldn't really handle anything else at the moment. It was bad enough trying to work. He said he'd wait forever if need be. Christ, he's either the sweetest man in the world or the stupidest!

Desperate Measures

Monday 3rd June

'Matt, are you all right. You didn't do anything, did you?'

'About what, Charlie?'

'You know . . . Shane and all that.'

'Why? Has something happened?'

'He dumped me tonight, that's all. He said I was a stupid little f-ing kid.'

'That's a result. I hope you're pleased.'

'I don't like to be called stupid.'

'For Christ's sake, Charlie, you can't have it all bloody ways.'

'Oh, hi Mum.'

'You can't have *what* all ways?'

'Nothing. I was just talking to Matt about my exams.'

From: 'Matt' <mattmason@coolmail.com>
Date: Monday 3rd June
To: hans@coolmail.com
Subject: Charlie and Goodall

You're never going to believe this, but I
think I sorted Charlie's problem. I must
have taken the crazy pill. I caught up with
that slimy bastard, Goodall, at break today
and told him that we all knew he was the
largest supplier of puff and E to the
school, and that I'd expose him with loads
of witnesses in PANTS if he didn't leave my
sister alone. Christ, I don't know how I
got through it. He thought it was dead
funny at first, and said that he didn't
give a toss about our stupid little paper,
but then, when I told him it was about to
become official, he changed his tune big
time. I was shitting myself because I
couldn't find anyone with enough balls to
back me up. Luckily, he swallowed it whole.
He then threatened to do me over, but I
told him that the piece was already written
and that if anything happened to me it
would be out before the bruises came up.

  Your old, still-in-one-piece, mate,
  Matt

Monday 3rd June

I'm sure something's happened. Charlie was like a different person over supper. I think whatever the problem was, it might have solved itself. One day I'll find out what it was all about.

Maybe now is the time to mention what Jim suggested, while we're all one big happyish family. I know it won't last. Trouble is, although I'd love to be with Jim all the time, I don't really want to leave this little house. I'm well aware that his is big and beautiful (the house, that is), but I've made this place mine and I'm not sure I want to give up my new-found independence yet. The trouble with Jim is that he's so reasonable and understanding. I almost wish he'd just tell me what to do. In a way it would take the responsibility off me. Is that girlie or what?

From: 'Matt' <mattmason@coolmail.com>
Date: Monday 3rd June
To: hans@coolmail.com
Subject: Jodie

Hi Hans,
Thanks for the tips on the great advance on Jodie. I hope you realise if you're wrong I'll be forced to bomb

Germany. I didn't really tell you what happened on Saturday. It was just us two in her room all afternoon. Luckily it was pissing down outside, so we didn't have to go anywhere (or spend money). It was so cool. Trouble is, when it got to make your mind up time, I lost my bottle and backed off. I know you reckon you should just go for it and see what happens, but I blew it. What if she'd told me to get lost? Do you reckon she's actually waiting for me to go first? Either way, I can't let it go on too long or she'll think I don't fancy her, or I'm gay . . . or worse.

Oh yeah, I meant to ask you, what's the music scene over Germany way? I don't think I've ever heard of a German band of any description except that old Seventies bunch Kraftwerk.
Matt

Modesty Prevails

'Hi Matt, it's Jodie.'

'Oh hi, I wasn't expecting you to phone.'

'I was worried. I just wanted to know what you decided to do about your sister. Are you all right?'

'Apart from the life-support machine and the grub in intensive care.'

'Be serious for a sec. What happened?'

'Nothing much. I just had a few words in the right places.'

'Look, I'm talking about you. Did he threaten you? I've heard about this guy from a couple of mates at my school.'

'He probably supplies your lot as well. I just pointed out a few things that he wouldn't want made public – if you know what I mean.'

'What did Charlie say?'

'She doesn't know I did anything. All she knows is that he dumped her.'

'Blimey, Matt, it's a bit brave.'

'Not really. I didn't think I had much choice.'

'Sometimes a man's gotta do what a man's gotta do – eh!'

'Are you taking the piss?'

'No, honest. I think it's cool. Anyway, I wanted to talk to you about your mum and my dad.'

'What about them?'

'Well, my dad told me the other night that he's in love with your mum and he's asked her to marry him.'

'WHAAH? Is he stark, raving bonkers? Do they do weddings in loony bins?'

'Don't be horrible. Anyway, your mum told him no apparently.'

'Christ Almighty, they're both mad.'

'She said that she wasn't ready.'

'Ready for what?'

'Not *that*, if that's what's churning through your grubby brain. I'm sure they went there ages ago.'

'This is all too much for me.'

'Me too. If they did get married, presumably they'd want to live together.'

'I believe I've heard of such things. Disgusting, isn't it?'

'Don't be silly, I'm serious. It would make you my step-brother.'

'You mean your silly step-brother. Flipping hell, Jodie, what does that mean? Does that mean we couldn't – like . . .?'

'Here you go again. Don't start getting ideas.'

'Still, it wouldn't be so far to see you, would it? Your mum's only round the corner.'

'That's nothing, I spend nearly every weekend at Dad's. I think I'd better change the locks on my room now, just in case.'

'Hang on, I'll just go get my chopper.'

'That's enough of that sort of talk.'


```
From: 'Matt' <mattmason@coolmail.com>
Date: Tuesday 4th June
To: hans@coolmail.com
Subject: Moving Maybe
```

Are you sitting down? Be prepared for the awesomest news ever. You really are never, ever — ever, never (ever) going to believe this. That Jim bloke — the one that goes out with my mum (for want of a better phrase) has told Jodie he wants to marry her — not Jodie . . . my mum. Not only that, but the silly moo's gone and turned him down. Do you realise the horrendous implications of this act of gross selfishness? If my ma marries him, we'd all have to move in together. Are you with me or ahead of me? How bad would that be on a scale of one to ten? Talk about babe on the premises alert. Her Jodiness spends almost every weekend with her old man, apparently. She'd NEVER be able to go out with anyone else then. What d'you think? Anyway, as I said, my stupid mother's turned him down.

This calls for deviousness on a scale not yet known to man. Somehow I've got to get my old lady to change her mind, without her guessing where I'm coming from.

Sorry to hear about Steffi. She looked pretty gorge equipment from the pic. How do you do it? I couldn't believe she was a proper German with dark hair and all. Why did she dump you? You didn't show her your . . . no, even you wouldn't have done that. Anyway, fear not. The way you carry on, it'll be like buses. There'll be another one along in a minute (or less in super-efficient Germany).

Tuesday 4th June

I've been worried ever since I turned Jim down that he might begin to look elsewhere. Got the distinct feeling he's one of those people who can't bear to be alone. Therein lies the problem. I also got the distinct feeling I might be the sort of person who can't bear to live with anyone (especially Matt). Having said that, if I had to, it would be with someone like Jim. Going to have to talk about it with the kids. Don't know whether to mention Jim's house yet. The minute they hear about indoor swimming pools and snooker rooms the job will be done. Maybe I'll tackle it when I get back from Kate's hen night tomorrow (or maybe I won't).

To Move or Not to Move?

'Matt. Could you spare a minute? I've got something to ask you.'

'Uh?'

'I have to talk to you. It's important.'

'Oh no. What have I done now, Mum?'

'It's about Jim.'

'What about him? Have I said something wrong or something?'

'No, nothing like that. I sort of wanted to ask your advice.'

'My advice? Blimey. I've only met him twice.'

'He's asked me to marry him.'

'I – um – know.'

'You know? How?'

'Jodie told me.'

'What did she say?'

'She said you said no.'

'Oh, I see. What did you say?'

'He didn't ask me, did he?'

'Don't be silly. What did you say to Jodie?'

'I said it's up to you.'

'Did she say any more than that?'

'She said he wants us all to move to his house.'

'What did you think about that? Sorry, what *DO* you think about that?'

'Don't know really. Could be cool.'

'You're not just saying that because you'd see more of Jodie?'

'No.'

'Are you sure?'

'Yeah. Anyway, I thought she lives with her mum.'

'Yes, but she spends practically every weekend with her dad. Could you handle that?'

'Suppose so. What does Charlie think?'

'I thought I'd ask you first.'

'Blimey. Where does he live – this Jim?'

'At Sandhills, by the golf course. It might mean changing schools.'

'So what? One crap school's as good as another.'

'I haven't even told Jim I'm considering it, but I suppose if I said yes – sorry, *we* said yes – it could be fairly soon.'

'Has he got room?'

'Oh plenty. He's got a huge house, with a swimming pool and a snooker room and everything. He's the executive producer for about three series.'

'Bloody hell, I didn't realise he was that loaded.'

'It's not because of that, Matt. I said we were all right as we are. What do you think?'

'Does it really matter what I think?'

'I wouldn't be asking if it didn't.'

'Can I think about it for a while?'

'Of course, darling. It's a big move.'

'What's a big move? Where's he going, Mum?'

'Oh hi, Charlie. I'm glad you're here. I've just been discussing something with your brother.'

'You two haven't had another row?'

'Jim's asked me – or rather us – to move in with him.'

'Flipping hell. When?'

'Whenever. We didn't discuss it. I said no.'

'Don't you want to, Mum?'

'I don't know. I think Jim's wonderful, but I was just thinking of you two.'

'Mum says he's got a huge house with a swimming pool and a snooker room.'

'I don't think that should be a consideration, Matt. What do you think, Charlie? I've just told your brother, it might mean moving schools.'

'It's all a bit sudden, Mum.'

'Well, we don't have to hurry.'

From: 'Matt' <mattmason@coolmail.com>
Date: Wednesday 5th June
To: hans@coolmail.com
Subject: All Change

You know I'm always banging on that you're never going to believe stuff. Well this time you so really aren't. Things are moving très fast at Château Mason. Charlie and I have officially been asked what we think about going to live with this guy Jim — and Mum of course. Not only will I be just round the corner to her Jodiness, but she'll be coming to stay with her father — AND ME — nearly every bloody weekend!!!!!!!

I can see all the downsides that you pointed out. You're right, but I can't worry about them now, can I? Bird in the hand, after all. Anyway, Mum said it might mean me being released from school. It's got to be better to be pulled out than thrown out! Talk about timing.

Oh, did I mention this guy Jim lives in a huge house with a swimming pool (inside, of course) and a snooker room? Oh yes, and Mum's just told me he's got a place in the South of France. Christ, I think I'LL marry him if she doesn't.

Being a fully paid up socialist, you will realise, of course, that all this opulence will make no difference to my politics whatsoever. As long as my mother is happy, then I am prepared to sacrifice myself. (That's odd, I have this strange sensation that my nose is growing.)

Seriously, it could be great. I'll be able to attack the privileged classes from an equal position, ha ha. There's no better socialist than a rich one I always say. Only joking.

Sorry I've been banging on. I never asked you — how was your weekend in Munich? Did your Mum and Dad allow you to get schtuck into ze beer? I've heard it runs from the taps out that way. I wish you could e-mail beer. I'd be rat-arsed every night. Is it true that the average consumption of beer in Germany is 137 litres per person per year (I got that off the Net)? There must be some very pissed babies over your way.

Anyway, here's hoping I'll soon be too severely posh to talk to the likes of you.

Bye for now,

Matt

Wednesday 5th June

I don't believe it. I'm in a sort of family-induced daze. I thought telling the kids my plans was going to lead to a long, drawn-out battle, probably ending in defeat. This is a bit like winning the war without having a fight. Trouble is, I'd almost hoped they'd point blank refuse – it would have made my decision so much easier. Now I'm more worried than I was before – especially about Matt. I know exactly where he's coming from. He just can't believe he'll have his Jodie on tap. Therein lies the disaster. What'll happen when they aren't love's young dream any more – which is inevitable? It would be a total nightmare. I must have this out with Jim. The very thing that would have made it easy is the very thing that could make it impossible. Had a feeling this might all turn out to be too good to be true.

Seen at the Pictures

'Matt, can I come in? It's me, Charlie.'

'Hang on a sec, I'll clear some space.'

'Jesus, how do you find anything in here?'

'Easy-peasy. I just wait until things die and then sniff 'em out. What's up?'

'I really don't know if I should be telling you this. But I feel I might owe you one.'

'You're not still having trouble with that Goodall bloke?'

'No, nothing like that. I saw your Jodie last night – that's all.'

'Jodie? Where? Are you sure?'

'Sure I'm sure. It was at the movies. Me and Daisy went to see the latest Austin Powers thing. She was in the row in front.'

'Oh yeah, who with?'

'She was with this bloke. Look, I'm sorry, Matt. I could have just ignored it, but they really looked like an item.

119

Me and Daisy followed them for a bit after the film. He drives one of those flash new scooters – the BMW one.'

'Oh well, that's how it is. So what, I say?'

'Don't you care?'

'Why should I? Plenty more where she came from.'

'I wish I hadn't had to tell you, but I didn't want you making a fool of yourself.'

'Me, why? She can do what she bloody wants. See if I care.'

Saturday 8th June

Poor old Matt. Charlie's just told me about Jodie and the other boy. Haven't actually seen Matt since she told him. She said he didn't appear to give a damn, but I don't believe it. He's holed up in his room, grunting whenever I try to talk to him. Poor kid, I remember how it all felt when I was his age. It's as if the whole world's closed in. But it was an accident waiting to happen. For one minute I really thought that it might be possible for Jim and me to live together in the near future. How stupid could I be? How could I have thought that our future happiness could ever depend on the stability of my teenage son's first proper relationship?

Better tell Jim as soon as possible. Damn! Why do these things always happen to me (or am I just being selfish?).

From: 'Matt' <mattmason@coolmail.com>
Date: Saturday 8th June
To: hans@coolmail.com
Subject: Jodie From Hell

Bum, balls and bugger! Please forgive the blood-stained e-mail, I've just cut my throat. Just found out that Jodie's seeing another bloke, the cow. Charlie told me. Can you believe it? The great romance of my life is all but over, and I haven't even snogged her yet (let alone anything else). I bet it's because I was too flipping slow off the mark. She probably thought I wasn't interested, stupid bitch! Charlie told me she'd seen her at the movies with this bloke who had a scooter. One of those poncy BMW scooter things with the roof bit that goes right over the top. Still, I suppose it beats a clapped-out mountain bike.

Sorry, Hans, I just thought I'd e-mail you before I die. As you probably have guessed, I haven't really cut my throat — far too hurty and I can't stand blood. But please suggest an alternative method. What's big in Germany? I'd like something that might get into the papers so she'd have to see it. Christ, it wouldn't take much to get into our local paper — they're still running 'cat stuck up trees' stories. Please reply soon, otherwise I might go off the idea.

Bye for now. Oh, by the way, how are you?

Matt

Jodie Who?

'Ah, Matt, darling, you've come down at last. Are you all right, sweetheart?'

'Uh!'

'I asked if you were all right. I'm sorry about what happened.'

'Oh yeah! What did happen?'

'You know, with Jodie.'

'Oh her.'

'Do you want to talk about it?'

'Not particularly. Why should I?'

'Perhaps you should talk to her.'

'Why?'

'Perhaps you should ring her and ask where you stand.'

'What for?'

'I thought you liked her.'

'She's all right.'

'Well?'

'There's plenty of others. Look, stop making a fuss, Ma.'

123

'Maybe she ought to be allowed to explain.'

'Why? She doesn't have to explain anything. Look, I don't care.'

'C'mon Matt, I'm on your side. Don't shut me out again.'

'What d'you mean?'

'I thought we'd been getting along a bit better.'

'Maybe *you* had.'

'I just don't see why we always have to be at loggerheads.'

'What are they when they're at home?'

'It's just an expression. You know what I mean.'

'Do I?'

'Yes, you do. You're just trying to be difficult. Just because you're fed up , there's no need to take it out on me. You should do a bit of growing up.'

'And you should do a bit of getting off my case. Look, Ma, when I want your opinion I'll ask for it. I'm going back upstairs.'

'Don't you want anything to eat before I go out?'

'No.'

From: 'Matt' <mattmason@coolmail.com>
Date: Saturday 8th June
To: hans@coolmail.com
Subject: Dying

Christ, I'm starving. I went downstairs and got the third degree from Mum about the Jodie sitch, lost my temper and then came up without anything to eat. Now I feel bloody stupid. I can't go down again — I'd look even stupider. Got any spare frankfurters you could e-mail across, before I die? I suppose I was a bit hard on Ma. She means well but somehow she always manages to get on my tits. She reckons I should ring Jodie and have it out, but I think that'd be so uncool. Anyway, I told her I didn't care. If Jodie wants to screw every bloke in the area, that's not my bloody problem, is it?

Thanks for the advice on my approaching suicide. You really are a pal. I particularly liked the version where I jump out of the top floor of the local newspaper office and go splat on the pavement in front of their main entrance. The trouble is they've just moved to a new single-storey office on the industrial estate.

More possible, I thought, was the stabbing-myself-to-death-on-Mum's-TV-show idea — that would cheer it up a bit. Trouble is, Mum once said it only goes out almost live. Knowing my current luck, they'd have a thirty-second loop just to clear up any stiffs. They must poison a few on a cookery show.

The best one I came up with was to starve myself to death, but so far I've only missed one meal by half an hour and I'm going off the idea big time. Perhaps I'll just eat myself to death instead. Yes, I'll do that. What's the opposite to anorexia. Fat-bastardexia?

Matt

Saturday 8th June

Just as I thought – the little so and so's clammed up again. I suppose, thinking about it, I'm the last person he'd talk to. I think he even resents the fact that I even know about the Jodie business. Maybe it's all a 'cool' thing with Matt. He just doesn't want anyone to know how devastated he really is. Now he's gone back to his room without any supper, just to make a point, and as he does so the Cold War descends on the house again. Either way, I was obviously wrong about the progress I thought we were making.

I bet I find out what's going on – it's hard not to when I'm seeing the girl's father. I think it's best to just leave it alone, on consideration. Talked for hours with my girlfriend, Lindy, about it this evening. She said her kids were just the same and they only snapped out of it when they went to university. I really don't know if I can stand it for that long.

A Call From the Past

'Hello, who's that?'

'Charlie.'

'Hi, Charlie? Could I speak to Matt? It's Jodie.'

'Oh, Jodie. Hi. Hang on, I'll just call out and see if he's in.'

'Matt, are you in? It's Jodie on the jellibone.'

'Tell her I'm not . . . Oh hell . . . all right, tell her to hang on.'

'Hello.'

'Hi, Matt, it's Jodie.'

'Oh – er – hi.'

'You were going to call me last night.'

'Oh yeah? I forgot.'

'You forgot – oh I see. Is anything wrong?'

'No, nothing.'

'Are you sure?'

'No. Why should there be?'

'You sound different – all sort of arsy.'

'So what? Why should you care?'

128

'Hang on a mo – what's wrong? Has someone been talking about me?'

'Maybe.'

'Who was it?'

'Nobody you know.'

'So, what am I supposed to have done?'

'Oh nothing. Look, I'm a bit busy at the moment.'

'Wait a minute, Matt. What are you all pissed off about?'

'Look, nothing. I just would have liked to have known you've got another bloody boyfriend.'

'What the hell are you talking about? Oh, hang on. You don't mean Simon, do you?'

'How should I know what his bloody name is, and why the hell are you laughing?'

'Simon's my ex-boyfriend.'

'*Ex*-boyfriend?'

'Yeah, I hadn't seen him for ages. Not face to face, anyway. We're quite good mates now, on the phone. I suppose someone saw us together last week. We went to the movies – for old times' sake. He's had another girlfriend for over six months.'

'Well, that's nice . . . Right then – Bye.'

'Hang on. Why are you being so bloody childish?'

'Oh so sorry. I'm always like this. It's genetic.'

'Not since I've known you.'

'Perhaps you don't know me that well.'

'I certainly didn't realise you were so flipping possessive.'

'Look, you can do what you bloody want.'

'See! We're not even going out and you're getting all uptight because I see other people.'

'That's fine if you want to. I'll see you around some time. Bye.'

'Hey! Wait a sec, why are you being like this? Matt . . . Matt . . . are you there? . . . Matt!'

```
From: 'Matt' <mattmason@coolmail.com>
Date: Sunday 9th June
To: hans@coolmail.com
Subject: Jodie Again
```

Thanks for last night's e-mail. Jodie rang me about an hour ago and I did the old treat-'em-mean-keep-'em-keen bit on the phone like you suggested and she got all upset. She said that the bloke she was with was her ex-boyfriend and that she hadn't seen him for ages. Then I went all sort of dismissive, pretending I didn't give a shit and then put the phone down. I feel bloody awful. It makes me feel sick thinking about her with someone else. Do you really think it was her ex? I can almost see you shaking your head. What if she doesn't phone back? What a solid-gold disaster that would be.

She said I was getting all possessive and that we weren't even going out. How uncool does that make me sound — the guy who can't even build up the courage to snog, telling a wicked-looking babe who she should and shouldn't go to the movies with? Is that about as pants as it can get, or what?

And another thing. What's going to happen with this moving business? I'm going to look a right dickhead going to live with her dad when I'm not even talking to her. I bet Mum will go through the roof when I tell her I'm not going . . . ever. Sorry mate, I've been ranting on for just about ever. Haven't asked anything about ze Fräuleins for ages.

Let me know what or 'who' you're up to on the next mail.

All the best,

Matt

Sunday 9th June

That's just about it. Matt just told me, as calmly as you like, that he won't ever be coming to live at Jim's house. I was really cross – lost it completely. I didn't even get round to telling him I've decided against it anyway. He said if me and Charlie wanted to go, he'd stay here in the house with the dog. What a brilliant idea that would be. He can't even look after a small room, let alone a house, and as for poor old Elvis, he'd be dead within a couple of weeks from malnutrition. I bet Charlie'll go through the roof. She's talked of nothing else. She's even been planning her room at Jim's place. Still, I suppose it means I don't have to tell her that it's my decision.

Bloody kids. It's not fair. All they do is take, take, take. They never consider what we adults might be feeling. It makes me sick. It was all right for John. He just upped and left when he felt like it – the bastard.

World War Three

Monday 10th June

'Matt, could you come down? I have to talk to you . . .

'Matt, did you hear me, I know you're up there. Please come down . . .

'Matt, for Christ's sake, get down here now, you're making me very angry . . .

'Oh, there you are. You could have answered me.'

'Uh?'

'OK Matt, I've had just about enough of this. How long are you going to be playing the damned Heartbreak Kid? I don't think we can stand it much more.'

'I'm not playing anything. I told you I don't bloody care.'

'Look, I said I was sorry about what happened between you and Jodie the other day, but Jim said she rang to explain and you gave her the big brush-off.'

'Look, I asked you before to get off my case. It's my business.'

'It's mine if you make the whole house miserable.'

'You don't understand anyway.'

'Oh don't I? Oh don't I, young man? Oh no, of course, I've never been your age, have I? I was born aged thirty flipping nine, was I? D'you think I've never been dumped by a boy – or been two-timed? How do you think I felt when your dad walked out, eh? That's just it, you didn't bloody think, did you? It was just you, you, you, like always. How is this all affecting you? I bet that's all you thought about. It's all you ever think about.'

'No one ever asked me about anything.'

'No one ever asked you, did you say? It couldn't just be because you always make out you don't want to know anything, could it? Now you're saying, I should have come along, made an appointment and told you how sorry I was to have inconvenienced your life, by pissing off your father so much that he went and found someone else. Is that how it should have gone? Is it?'

'I didn't mean that.'

'Well, what is it then? The trouble is you think being a parent is dead easy. Just dishing out rules and providing food. Let me tell you this, you selfish little so and so, I've never had any training for bringing up a grumpy, insolent teenager – this is a first for me too. Do you ever think of that? Kids aren't like washing machines, you know. You don't get a set of instructions – or a guarantee. And you can't send them back if you're fed up with them. To make a house work it takes effort on all sides, and so far all the effort has come from me and I'm seriously fed up with it – and you! All you do is leave your stupid moods around for the rest of us to gingerly step round or trip over. Well, I've had enough. I love Jim and I was given a chance to live with him and be happy ever after. But, unlike you, I have to consider everyone else, right down to the sodding dog. OK if it doesn't happen now, because of your stupid spat with Jodie, then I'll just have to wait, but don't think I don't resent you for it.'

'I – I –'

'You – you what? Why don't you just go back to your filthy den and think about what I said. Supper will be in an hour. After that, this particular maid's taking the night off. OK? While I'm out, if you've got time, you might consider growing up a bit.'


```
From: 'Matt' <mattmason@coolmail.com>
Date: Monday 10th June
To: hans@coolmail.com
Subject: Mad Mother Alert!!!


Action stations a go-go! The house is like
a bloody war-zone. Just because I said to
Mum that I wasn't ever moving, and just
because she'd heard that Jodie had rung me
and I'd given her the heave-ho, she looked
```

like was going to clobber me. Blimey, I could have been a badly battered boy.

Why is it you always think of what to say when it's too late. What I should have said during the great shout-in was that I had never actually asked to be born into this family. It wasn't my fault that I ended up living with her and Charlie. And another thing. If she hadn't got involved with my dad I could have been someone else's. Does it work like that? Anyway, I should have said all that, shouldn't I?

Just as things are getting better with Charlie, I've managed to upset everyone else. Not only have I pissed Mum off, but I've managed to piss off Jodie and her dad as well. I think I'll just ring up my dad and piss him off too — and his bloody girlfriend. Then I'll have done the lot apart from you and Elvis. Job done.

I'm going round to Dean's for a beer or thirty.

Thanks for reading all this crap.

Take care,

Matt

Monday 10th June

Crikey, what came over me? I completely lost it and gave Matt both barrels right between the eyes. His face drained of colour. I've never seen anything like it. I don't think anyone has ever spoken to him like that. Heaven knows how he's going to be when I see him again. Part of me really wants to apologise, but I'm well aware that would be fatal. He'd be able to run right over me whenever he felt like it.

Now the dust has settled, half of me thinks that me and Charlie should go and live with Jim and leave Matt to it, despite my decision. He'll come running as soon as all his clothes are dirty or he's emptied the fridge. Unfortunately, I don't think you can do that sort of thing. You'd get done for desertion or abandonment or something.

Poor Matt must be feeling pretty much out on a limb. He's now upset just about everyone. I wonder if he's got the courage to come out of his room and face me. If he does, I'll maybe say I'm sorry for going off on one.

Who's Sorry Now?

Tuesday 11th June

'Mum, have you got a sec?'

'Oh it's you, Matt. I'm surprised you're still talking to me. Look, before you say anything, I think I went a little overboard last night. I'm not apologising for everything, but I'm afraid I lost it.'

'Yeah, it was about that. Look, I think that I . . . well, I think that you might have been a bit right.'

'A *bit* right. About what?'

'Me.'

'Oh really. I said a lot, which bit did you mean?'

'I suppose all of it really. I think I might have been a bit selfish. I – er . . .'

'Go on . . .'

'It's just that I . . . It's just that I really – um – messed up with Jodie, and I suppose I was taking it out on you, sort of thing.'

'So?'

'So I'm sorry, all right. Sometimes I hate just about everybody and feel everyone's picking on my case.'

'I think that might be an age thing, darling.'

'The thing is, it'll probably happen again. I almost want to say sorry in advance.'

'Like a warranty kind of thing. I promise, should I lose my temper I don't mean it.'

'You're taking the mickey now.'

'No Matt, I promise. I think I understand. What you're really telling me is that whatever you say, it's just dictated by the mood you're in. Maybe I should try a little harder to understand that too.'

'I reckon.'

'I've just been thinking about Jodie as well and I think you should do exactly what you've just done with me. Don't go over the top, but just explain that it was all a bad mood thing, and say you're sorry.'

'She'll probably tell me to get lost.'

'If she really likes you, she'll come round – but not necessarily immediately.'

'Not necessarily ever.'

'It happens to all of us. I seem to remember that it was much worse when I was your age. These days I seem to take things as they come, thank God.'

'I wish I could. I seem to be thinking about Jodie all the time. You must think I'm bonkers.'

'Not at all, but talking about it can really help. We are on the same side really. I think you forget that sometimes.'

Tuesday 11th June

I can't believe it. I never thought I'd see it – Matt apologising. It was strange – I really felt sorry for him. He said that he hardly knows when he's being horrible. He said he sometimes thinks everyone's picking on him. Poor kid sounded really miserable. I can't really help him because he thinks parents are from another planet, but I just can't let this opportunity slip. And then there's the Jodie situation. From what Jim says she's still spitting feathers, but he's not sure whether it's about what Matt said, or whether it was something to do with the other boy.

```
From: 'Matt' <mattmason@coolmail.com>
Date: Tuesday 11th June
To: hans@coolmail.com
Subject: Catch This
```

Phew, I actually said I was sorry to Mum. She said I should do the same to Jodie, but I pretended not to take it in. I really need to think about that one.

What did you think of the latest PANTS? Have you read it yet? With all this stuff going on, I haven't really done very much. I think I'm going to write a bit on how crap telly's getting. Do you get things like Pop Idol and Big Brother over in Germany? I reckon if I see another one of them I'll kick the screen in.

Please report back,

Matt

Sorry Really Is the Hardest Word

Wednesday 12th June

'Oh hello, is that Jodie's mum? It's Matt Mason.'

'Oh, hello Matt.'

'Is Jodie there?'

'I'll just see if she's in. Hang on a sec.'

'Hello.'

'Hi, it's Matt.'

'Oh you. What do *you* want?'

'I just wanted to talk. I think I've been a bit of a prat.'

'A *bit* of a prat?'

'All right. A lot of a prat.'

'You're not kidding. I swore I'd never talk to you again.'

'Please don't be like that. Look, I've said I'm sorry.'

'You haven't actually.'

'Oh no – I – er – right. Look, I'm sorry, all right. I just do such stupid things sometimes.'

'I thought you were really childish. Haven't you ever had a girlfriend before?'

'Yeah, loads.'

'Loads?'

'Well, not loads, that's a slight porkie. Not many at all really.'

'How many?'

'Well, when I really count up it's sort of . . . er . . . oh OK, sort of – er – none.'

'Does that mean you haven't . . . ?'

'Oh hell! No, if you must know.'

'Good, nor have I.'

'Really? You seem so . . .'

'Of course I haven't. What sort of a girl do you think I am?'

'A bloody good one if you want to know. I've been thinking about you non-stop. I just couldn't think of a way of saying what a plonker I've been.'

'It takes quite a bit to say sorry. Even for a plonker.'

'You're not bloody kidding. I seem to make a habit of it. I had to say sorry to my mum the other day.'

'What about? I'm always falling out with mine.'

'I'd prefer not to say. It was to do with you as well.'

'What have I got to do with your mum?'

'Quite a bit, if you think about it. She'll be your wicked stepmother if she ever marries your dad.'

'Blimey, I hadn't thought of that.'

'I couldn't bear coming to your dad's house, if you weren't speaking to me.'

'We should make a pact, Matt.'

'What sort of pact?'

'We should make a pact that whatever happens to us – you know – we should try to stay mates.'

'Easier said than done. But I'll go for it.'

'Good, now, what sort of week have you had?'

'Bloody terrible, thanks.'

'So have I. It's dead hard staying cross.'

'Do you feel better now?'

'A bit. But you're still on probation. If you give me a hard time like that again, I'm off – or you're off.'

'What about the pact?'

'Oh yeah, I forgot. OK, it will mean we can never be more than friends.'

'Does that mean we are now then?'

'Well, that all depends, doesn't it?'

'On what?'

'That would be telling.'

'When can I see you again?'

'Did I say you could?'

'Please, Jodie, don't play games. I did say I was sorry.'

'OK, maybe at the weekend. I'll ring you.'

From: 'Matt' <mattmason@coolmail.com>
Date: Wednesday 12th June
To: hans@coolmail.com
Subject: The Apology Kid

Just rang Jodie . . . and she almost forgave me. Thank God for that. Thinking about it, I suppose it gives the all-clear for the big family move west to Mum's bloke's place. Sounds like a cowboy film, doesn't it? It is odd, but I'm not sure Mum's so set on it now. I can't keep up.

It's dead weird, I seem to be getting on with everyone at this precise moment — even old Phillips at school. I showed him my piece on the state of telly for PANTS and he wants to put a cleaned-up version in for the school essay prize. Me, up for a prize — I so don't think so. He said he agreed with me completely and that it was about time young people started complaining about the sort of dumbing-down bollocks that they're being served up. Not his words, mind you. I'll attach the piece on to the end of this e-mail so you can see what you think.

If only I could get this worked up about school. You sound as if you're doing all right over there. How the hell do you do it? I even tried quite hard in Maths the other night, and I still couldn't get my head round it. It's like speaking another language. Maybe I'm like those people who can't see their words right. Dickslexic, I think they call it (or is that people who can't see their willies?).

Please inform,

Matt

From: 'Matt' <mattmason@coolmail.com>
Date: Wednesday 12th June
To: hans@coolmail.com
Subject: Hilda

Thanks for correcting my spelling (but dickslexic was a joke). And thanks for the jpeg of your new mate Hilda. How do you do it? I reckon you're cutting the pics out of magazines. Either that or you're on a winning streak. She looks about eighteen. Don't tell me she is? That'd make you a toyboy. If I didn't have Jodie (which I almost didn't) I'd be out there with you. Extremely good work.

By the way, I forgot to add on the bit

that I wrote about telly for PANTS. You'll
find it attached to this e-mail.

Is telly the same in Germany, Hans? I
really need to know. Could you do a little
bit on it for us?

Take care,

Matt

Wednesday 12th June

*Thank the Lord. Matt's just told me he's made it up with
Jodie . . . until the next time. He also said he didn't mind
moving and didn't even go off on one when I told him I'd
got second thoughts. I think he agreed it was all a bit
soon. I'm beginning to think it's important that Matt
stays at the same school, anyway.*

*Had that blasted French chef on the phone again
today. He really won't give up. He says he has just sold
the idea of a programme set in the village in France
where he was brought up – a sort of triumphant return,
kind of thing. His mother's in her eighties, apparently,
and taught him everything he knows. Wants me to work
with him on the show. Shame, it could be excellent telly,
but I think it's safer to say no.*

Matt's Surprise

Friday 14th June: *breakfast*

'Ah, Matt, I've been meaning to ask you how your paper's going – the one at school. You haven't mentioned it lately.'

'Well, I haven't been kicked out yet.'

'Have you had any more warnings?'

'The opposite really. Old Phillips has put me up for a prize.'

'Prize? What sort of prize?'

'It's called the – er – the William What's-His-Face essay prize. I can't remember his name. Apparently some old codger, who used to go to our school in prehistoric times, left a load of dosh to be given out every year for the best essay.'

'But that's brilliant, Matt. I always knew you had it in you.'

'I didn't.'

'What was it about?'

'What?'

'The essay.'

'It was about telly and how crap I think it is.'

'Oh I see. I hope you didn't mention *Chefs at Home*.'

'I didn't, but I could have.'

'I didn't know you hated it that much. What's wrong with it?'

'I don't actually hate it, compared with all the other stuff. It's no worse than the rest of the cooking programmes.'

'Thanks a lot. That's almost a compliment. Seriously, darling, why don't you like it?'

'Do you really want to know? This could get nasty.'

'That's why I'm asking.'

'OK, are you sitting comfortably? Well, I think that in a world where over two-thirds of the people have to scrabble around for something to eat, poncing around like your chefs do is completely stupid and immoral.'

'Gosh. How do you mean – poncing around?'

'Oh, you know, fiddling about for yonks trying to make food look all arty on the plate and then going on about it like it really matters.'

'It's only supposed to be entertainment. Why do you take everything so seriously?'

'It's you lot that take it seriously. I always thought the main purpose of food was to keep us alive. Listening to some of those chefs you'd think they were making some great statement for art and mankind.'

'That programme helps keep our little family going, don't forget that.'

'That's not my fault, is it?'

'You'll learn one day that everything you do turns into a compromise.'

'You see, here we go again, Ma. You grown-ups always pull the when-you-get-to-my-age lever. Just because you've given in, why should I have to? I didn't make this flipping world, did I? You lot can compromise all you want, but count me out.'

'You wait till you've got a family to support, you might feel differently.'

'Oh Jesus, Mum – there you go again. Same old tune. You're just making excuses. Nobody made you have children. It's like saying that just because someone invented guns, we have to go around shooting each other all the time – it's bollocks!'

'That's ridiculous, it's nothing like that. People have to have children to keep the human race going.'

'Does that mean we have to have stupid cookery programmes in order to keep all those bloody chefs going – is that it?'

'You know it isn't. It's just that your attitude might soften when you have responsibilities.'

'I'll make a pretty crap journalist if I always go along with what the Great British Public thinks.'

'I think maybe we should stop now. This could get personal.'

'Good idea. Does that mean I won?'

'You just have to have the last word, don't you?'

'Of course.'

'See!'

'Of course.'

From: 'Matt' <mattmason@coolmail.com>
Date: Friday 14th June
To: hans@coolmail.com
Subject: Girls Again

Just had an argument with my ma this morning that didn't end in blood and tears — that's got to be a world record. Just as she was getting a pounding, she backed off and said we shouldn't push it. Not fair really, she was definitely getting the worst of it.

Only picked up your e-mail about five minutes ago. It must have got stuck somewhere over the Channel. Sounds like things are hotting up with Fräulein Hilda. Older girls sound muchos wickedos to me. Did she really try to get your old chap out? Blimey, mate, isn't that against the law over there? You don't want to get kicked out of ze Fatherland for that, do you? Mind you, you'd get maximum brownie points with the blokes at school. Deported

151

for gross sexual behaviour — cool or what?
You'd be carried through the airport
shoulder high.

Seriously, what are you going to do?
Matt

Friday 14th June

*New ground broken. Matt and I had a proper argument
and came away unscathed. If that boy didn't annoy me
so much I could almost respect him. Went on about*
Chefs at Home *and made a lot of sense. I can't ever
remember having been that idealistic. Where does he
get it from? He made his point so well that I was
fighting off being proud of him. Mind you, if you can't
believe in things at his age, why bother? Maybe it's
only the young that can have such purity of thought.
It's so difficult to argue with. What he can't
understand (and why should he?) is that, when it
comes right down to it, most people will do absolutely
anything to protect themselves and those most close to
them. It's simply a fact of life. It's true that most of us
sell out and give up.*

*He let me read the piece he wrote about television for
his newspaper. It was so clever and so funny. He went on
about the reality TV shows like 'Pop Idol' and 'Big
Brother', saying that ordinary people are offered the*

chance of stardom and money only to be humiliated when they lose. He then compared them to the Romans feeding Christians to the lions with the added dimension of the lions being interviewed to see what their victims tasted like. That's so bloody true. He then said that the last time they did stuff like that it led to the decline and fall of an empire. If he could just control his language, I reckon he could practically work as a journalist now. Thank God I've found something his father and I can encourage.

More and more I'm beginning to realise that my Matt might actually make something of himself after all. He believes practically nothing anyone tells him and is prepared to hang on like a dog with a bone, until he gets to what he is satisfied might be the truth. That's almost lawyer material. The trouble is, when you get to my age, you realise there is no real truth. What is true to one person is not necessarily true to another. I wouldn't even dare try to explain that to an idealistic fifteen-year-old.

Life is so black and white to someone like Matt and in a way I'm beginning to love him for it. Whatever next.

Later that day

'Matt, have you got a mo? I need to talk to you.'
'What about, Charlie? I'm a bit busy.'

'I've just been talking to Daisy.'

'So? What's that got to do with me?'

'She told me all about the Shane Goodall thing.'

'What about it?'

'She told me what you said to him.'

'Eh? How does she know?'

'He apparently told his mate Steve that you'd threatened him, and he was going to do you over.'

'Oh no he won't. I covered all that.'

'Why did you do it? I asked you not to get involved.'

'I don't really know.'

'I just wanted to say thank you. I didn't know you cared about me.'

'You're my sister, aren't you?'

'But we've always been horrible to each other.'

'Yeah, well.'

'Yeah, well, I think you're really brave.'

Charlie the Angel

'Hi Matt, have you been in long? What are you up to?'

'Oh hi, Charlie. Just trying to get my head round my Maths homework. I can't make any sense of it.'

'Let's have a look. It might be something we revised recently.'

'You sure? It's dead boring.'

'Seems a bit nerdy, but I don't actually find Maths boring. Maybe that makes me boring. I don't know.'

'It certainly ain't boring helping your poor little broth.'

'Do you really find studying hard?'

'It's not exactly hard. It's just that I can't keep my mind in one place for more than about fifteen seconds.'

'I used to be like that until I broke it all up into small packages.'

'Like how?'

'I set myself half-hour periods. I use my alarm clock. After each session I give myself a treat as a sort of reward, like a drink or a Mars Bar, or sometimes I make

155

a phone call or even watch a soap. Then I go back for more.'

'Does it work?'

'It seems to work for me – look at the results . . . and I'm not nearly as clever as you.'

'You whah? Christ, that's the nicest thing you ever said to me . . . and the daftest.'

'I mean it. I've just got a good method of working. It's like that old tortoise and hare story – you know – the one where the old tortoise (that's me) trudges on while the hare (that's you) keeps rushing past and taking a break, until one time he falls asleep and the tortoise plods past him and wins the race.'

'Surely it's the other way round? I keep plodding on and getting bloody nowhere, while you keep taking the breaks and keep winning.'

'Oh yeah, I never thought of it that way. Silly me. Anyway you should have a go at doing it my way. I bet it'll work. By the way, I read that thing you wrote on telly – Mum showed me. I thought it was brill.'

'What? I can't take all this praise. Are you building up to something? I don't owe you money, do I? It's not your birthday, is it?'

'No, I just thought you were right, that's all. Especially about all those pop star programmes. They build the kids to thinking their whole future's gonna be sorted out, simply to crush them and film them wallowing in their misery. It's sick – I hate it. The only people who make any money are those horrible arrogant bastards that present the crap. They're just bloody parasites.'

'Blimey, sis, I never thought you gave a damn. I thought you lived in a little pink bubble of your own.'

'It's because we've always been far too busy arguing. Mum told me about the pact you made with Jodie to sort of cool it when things got too heavy. I think it's a wicked idea.'

'It could make life a bit boringo.'

'Nothing's as boring as arguing all the time. It's so flipping destructive. You never get anywhere.'

'We'll turn into the Nice Family Robinson if we're not careful. Mind you, at least they won't want to make a telly programme about us. They only go for grumpy gits.'


```
From: 'Matt' <mattmason@coolmail.com>
Date: Saturday 15th June
To: hans@coolmail.com
Subject: Deep Shock!
```

Dear Hans,
Please come over to England immediately. I'm in severe need of being picked up off the floor. Charlie, my hitherto ghastly sister, just strolled in and had a proper

conversation with me in which we agreed about everything. Whaaaat!!!!! She even offered to help me with my homework. Whaaaat!!!! It's all too much. Just as I was recovering from all that, she said she thought I was cleverer than her. Can you believe it? Miss Never-Failed-An-Exam-In-Her-Life, Head-of-School, Light-of-the-World etc. accused me of being cleverer than her. I tell you, the world as I know it is going all arse-about-face and I'm not sure I'm ready. Next my dad'll be phoning up and telling me he's proud of me. Well, let's not go too far.

And then I got your e-mail. I was almost as gobsmacked about what you told me about the age of consent in Germany. Eighteen you say. Is it really true that nobody's allowed to do it until they're eighteen except — and this was the bit I couldn't get my head round — if they're married? Jeez, that's the only good reason for getting hitched I've ever heard of. I hope I got that right. Having said that, it could be a very expensive day out in the long run. Fifty years of misery for an early bonk.

I should imagine this might lead to

problems with your Hilda. You said she's
a year older than you. Does this mean that
when she gets to eighteen she'll have to
hang around for a year to try you out? Ha
ha, I don't think so, mein Herr. Mind
you, at the rate you get through girls,
you'll have had half of Germany by then -
and then you'll have to start on the men.
Sorry, it sounds that you really like
this Hilda a lot. I'm not really used to
that.

Aren't the consent laws bloody stupid?
Who's business is it apart from you and
your potential bonk — sorry — partner if
you want to get it on? If it's just about
getting preggers and being all responsible
and stuff, I wouldn't let half the
population of the world reproduce. If I
had my way, anyone wanting to have
children would have to pass a test to
prove basic intelligence. I'd start with a
joke or two, like that one 'What's pink
and wrinkly and hangs out your trousers?'
. . . answer — 'your mother'. Or the one
about the burglars that broke into the
police station and stole all the
toilets . . . the police had nothing to go
on. Boom, boom!

See if you can get hold of a German joke
or two and chuck them in your next e-mail.
Meantime I'm waiting for Jodie to phone. I
think she's making me suffer.

   Keep struggling,

   Matt

Saturday 15th June

*I can hardly believe it. I've just heard Charlie and Matt
chatting and giggling like kids in his room. I almost feel
left out. Makes such a change from trying to gouge each
other's eyes out. They used to be such sworn enemies.
Just goes to show that what Charlie told me last night
must have been true. She let me in on what had been
going on with this awful boy at school. I could hardly
believe it. My little Charlie. I knew she was in some sort
of trouble, but it was her best friend Daisy, apparently,
who found out that Matt had sorted the boy out.
Something about drugs, so she said. What an amazing
kid he is. He did it without anyone knowing – even
Charlie.*

   *Jim seemed to understand when I told him that we
wouldn't be moving in with him. He really is a sweetie. I
told him that it would be three years at the very most –
when both the kids are at university (I should be so
lucky?). I think Jim also needs a period of living by
himself – it will be a good test. If he can't stand it and*

160

starts to look for another partner straightaway, then it will answer its own question. Actually, I'm pretty sure it won't happen.

World of Pacts

Sunday 16th June: Matt's room

'Matt! Are you there? Can I come in?'

'Who is it?'

'Jodie.'

'Blimey, not half. Where did you come from? I didn't know you were coming round. I've been going mad waiting for you to phone.'

'I spoke to your mum earlier. She said you were actually doing homework. Can that be right? I thought I'd surprise you.'

'It must be more of a surprise to catch me doing homework.'

'Are you finding it any easier?'

'Yeah, almost. Charlie's been helping me with a few things. I think she should be a teacher, she's much better than the dead-beats we've got at school.'

'Dad told me that you lot won't be moving into the house.'

'Not yet anyway. I'm a bit pissed off about it.'

'Why's that?'

162

'You know why's that.'

'No I don't. Why should you want to move to our house so much?'

'Come on, are you trying to make me go red again?'

'It's not because of me, is it?'

'Course not, silly. It's because of the swimming pool and the snooker room.'

'Now you're calling me silly.'

'You know I don't mean it.'

'Show me you don't mean it.'

'What? How?'

'Blimey, Matt, do you have to have an instruction manual?'

'Oh I see. Oh shit . . .'

'Sorry – missed your chance. Now where were we . . . How are you getting on with your mum and Charlie?'

'Much better. We've done proper pacts at home like the one we talked about. You remember.'

'Yeah. How does that work for real?'

'It's dead simple. The first rule is that you have to stop an argument as soon as someone says the word *PACT*. The other rule is we have to change the subject or go away for at least half an hour before we can mention it again.'

'Like a cooling-off period.'

'Sort of.'

'Sounds brilliant, but what happens if you're in a right

strop, like I get in? I lose it big time, I warn you. I'd just want to say f-off and carry on.'

'Yeah, me too. But honest, Jodie, it really does calm things down. We've wasted so much bloody time arguing, and you come out with so many crap things when you're pissed off. Things you don't really mean.'

'Who *me*?'

'No, not you . . . I meant "one".'

'Do you need a cooling-off period now, Matt?'

'How do you mean?'

'I'll tell you, if something doesn't happen pretty soon, I'm going to boil over.'

'What? You mean . . . ?'

'Yeah, silly. Someone's got to snog someone round here sooner or later.'

'I never quite know when it's sort of right.'

'Does this seem right . . . '

'. . . Blimey.'

'Waiting for you was like waiting for the night bus.'

'Hang on, Jodie, I think I can see another one coming . . .'

' . . . Matt, stop, I can't do it when I'm laughing – I'll bloody suffocate.'

'Then I could really have my evil way with you.'

'You're sick. There's a word for people who fancy dead people.'

'At least they don't talk back, or giggle when you try

to kiss them. Anyway, I think I'd fancy you dead or alive.'

'What, like a highwayman.'

'Yeah – stand and deliver!'

'Like this . . .'

Sunday 16th June

Jodie's been in Matt's room for over an hour and there's not a sound. I reckon I'll have to break the door down soon to chuck a bucket of cold water over them. It's a bit strange imagining your little boy with a girl. It almost makes me sad. It's like the official end of childhood – like the last day of spring. Mind you, it looks as if it could also be the end of his stroppy phase and no one will be sorry to see the back of that. He mentioned his idea for an international paper for youngsters this morning and I think it's nothing short of brilliant. It's about time kids across the world got a chance to air their views, especially as grown-ups seem to be making a right mess of it.

From: 'Matt' <mattmason@coolmail.com>
Date: Sunday 16th June
To: hans@coolmail.com
Subject: Snoggerama!!!

Darling Hans (don't panic! I love everyone today),

It's happened! The eagle has landed. Snogged Jodie today and boy, it was awesome — even if she did make the first move. Christ, I reckon I'd be late for my own funeral. I now almost think it's better that we're not moving into her dad's house. I don't reckon I'd be able to think straight if she was there all the time. On top of that, I'd be watching her like a hawk . . . you know what I'm like. I told Mum this evening that I was on her side over all this business and she went all soppy and hugged me and nearly cried. Charlie's a bit pissed off, but she'll get over it. Even better, when Mum told me off about my room for the millionth time, I told her that my personal cleaner had died and got lost in there and that I couldn't find her anywhere. She looked like she was going to explode and then saw the funny side of it — thank God.

I'm not sure why, but I mentioned to old Phillips today about our plan to have an international students' internet magazine and he thought it was the brilliantest idea and that he'd see if any library funds could be made available to set it up. Maybe your school might be interested in sponsoring us. There's much more spare money over there, so you keep telling me.

You and I could be co-editors. We could have kids from all over the world telling us what a balls-up they think their parents are making of their country and the world. It could be fantastic — we'd be famous. Each month we could have a special subject, and invite opinions over the Net. They could e-mail us with their stuff. What do you think?

The weirdest thing is, that with all this going on — Jodie, and the paper and all — I can't wait to get up in the mornings. Who'd have ever thought it?

Onward and upward I say.

Matt

From: 'Matt' <mattmason@coolmail.com>
Date: Sunday 16th June
To: hans@coolmail.com
Subject: PANTS INTERNATIONAL

Heard a good joke about the Germans the other day which you might want to try out. Why do Germans only make fast cars? Because anything slower gets put in their horrible sausages.

I'm glad you're as excited as I am about PANTS INTERNATIONAL. I can't believe your dad's going to put some dosh into it — and maybe your school. Thanks for your invitation to ze Fatherland. We can all talk about it when I get there. Mum says she can probably pay the fare with her Sainsbury's air-miles. Not very cool — but hey! Do you think they make you wear something that says you're only travelling due to over-eating?

By the way, when I come, I promise I won't mention the war,

Be seeing you soon,

Matt

'Joseph, are you in there? It's me, your mother.'

Damn, I thought it might be that Jennifer Lopez again; she usually calls round about this time for a quick snog.

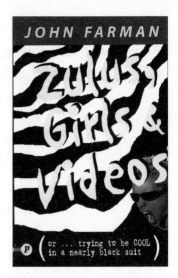

- **ZULUS** I always think my life's a bit like living in that old film *Zulu* – you know, the one where Michael Caine (me) and a bunch of rather hot British soldiers (Rover) are holding this garrison fort in Africa somewhere against thousands of ever-so-cross natives (my family).

- **GIRLS** This is really sad. One minute my head's full of the gorgeous, sexy Jade, and whether I might stand a chance with her after all, and the next, I'm thinking of dear sweet Lucy. Jade–Lucy, Lucy–Jade, I just can't get my brain straight.

- **VIDEOS** I'm a complete cinema junkie – a filmoholic – a movie maniac – a video voyeur, you name it. I don't know why, but all I ever think about is films (oh yes – and girls).

"Lively, witty text by a diverting writer." *Publishing News*

In the same series: *Merlin, Movies and Lucy Something
Sequins, Stardom and Chloe's Dad*

If you would like more information about books
available from Piccadilly Press and how to order
them, please contact us at:

Piccadilly Press Ltd.
5 Castle Road
London
NW1 8PR

Tel: 020 7267 4492
Fax: 020 7267 4493

Feel free to visit our website at
www.piccadillypress.co.uk